I0623029

BONNIE AND GUY

NOX SPACEY

THE WHUMPY PRINTING PRESS

ALSO BY NOX SPACEY

Magnanimous Moonrise & Savage Sunset

CONTENTS

Content Warnings   1

1. Chapter 1   2

2. Chapter 2   11

3. Chapter 3   17

4. Chapter 4   32

5. Chapter 5   36

6. Chapter 6   47

7. Chapter 7   61

8. Chapter 8   67

9. Chapter 9   81

10. Chapter 10   91

About the Author   103

Before You Go   104

— · —

Content Warnings

This story contains the following content:
- Animal attacks

- Broken bones

- Referenced character death

If this book isn't for you, no worries! But if it is, we hope you enjoy this story about a dragonrider and his unexpected ally...

1

The rest of Guy's unit was definitely very, very dead. But that was okay because he hadn't let himself get attached. Not attached at all! So really, it was fine that everyone was dead.

The mad howling of creatures up in the sky was less intense way down here amidst the wreckage on the pavement, but Guy knew better than to think he was safe. He was a sitting duck.

He probably would have been the only one in the unit who knew what a duck was since they'd been extinct for decades.

They'd all been kids. Well, not kids. Late teens, early twenties. Kids to *him*. He'd been the only one of the lot that had even been alive before the Tribulation, and honestly, he'd known as soon as he'd met them that they weren't going to last. So he hadn't gotten attached. Hadn't let himself get attached. Easy as that.

And then a building had fallen on their whole unit mid-flight, proving him right. He would rather be alive than right, which was part of the reason why he'd survived and the rest had died instantly when the massive, decrepit, vine-covered skyscraper had collapsed on top of them.

The only one he let himself get attached to these days was Bonnie, and even that seemed to be backfiring.

Explosions continued to sound in the distance on top of the echoing calls of roaring creatures, and Guy tried to extract himself from under Bonnie's flank where they'd fallen, anxiety mounting. Oh, his leg was definitely broken. Definitely definitely definitely. Bonnie had landed on her side and probably smashed his bones into a million pieces, pinning his leg to the cracked pavement. She wouldn't respond to his calls to get up.

"You have to get up, Bonnie." He choked back a sob, and tears blurred his vision. He needed her to get up. Not only because they would die if she didn't, but because he needed her. His sweet Bonnie. He'd raised her from almost the moment she'd hatched from her egg. His heart twisted seeing her pinned under the rubble of a Pre-Tribulation building.

The looming stone monuments of Pre-Tribulation cities were only good for serving as battlefields these days, and Guy hated them even more now that one had been pushed over on top of them all. The humans in the unit would definitely have died instantly; the dragons would still be alive, invulnerable to being killed by something as mundane as crushing concrete, but there would be no way to dig them out before the flock of Wellspring creatures could get to them for their next meal, so they were as good as dead.

Guy and Bonnie might be too. Bonnie was severely hurt from the fight, and they hadn't managed to clear the falling building in time, so they were now half-stuck under it. They were an easy meal for the starving, ravenous creatures swarming the city, and he could hear the leader of the attack calling for everyone to retreat. Even if they didn't die right here, right now, they were going to be left behind among the dead.

Bonnie was still alive, at least; he could tell by the laborious rising and falling of her sides. He slid his hand over her flank, feeling the softness of her powder blue feathers. The tears did spill over, then. "Bonnie. Bonnie-onnie, my sweet girl. Please. You have to get up, BonBon." He very gently tugged at the reins, which jingled with the motion. "Please."

He heard an infernal clicking behind him, and he craned his neck to see a pack of raptors picking their way over the rubble towards him, their huge talons scraping over the debris.

Those things weren't usually a problem. But then again, *usually* Guy was a hundred feet up in the air with the ability to just torch them in a cone of fire.

"Bonnie," he said, his voice pitching up with renewed urgency. "Bonnie, you have to get up, sweetheart. Please get up." He pressed his palm to her side again and pushed, trying to pry his leg out from under her.

Bonnie gave a labored, animalistic moan and started to writhe, claws grabbing at the air and tail thrashing, trying in vain to push the debris off herself.

4

"There you go," Guy encouraged. "There you go, girl."

The raptors had spotted him, though, and were now locked onto him, the pack making guttural clicks to call to each other.

"Faster," Guy squeaked. "Faster, Bonnie, faster, faster."

The raptors reached him before Bonnie could free herself. Their heads bobbed and cocked to the side to observe him.

"You can't eat me," Guy said, as though he had any chance of negotiating with them. "You don't want to kill me! I'm just some guy! Wait – wait!"

One of them lunged forwards and seized him by the arm he'd extended to shield himself, shaking its head savagely and pulling.

"Ow! Fuck! Fuck, fuck, stop! Ow!"

The rest of the pack pounced, then. So this was how he was going to die. It'd be a lie to say he wasn't disappointed. After all this, he'd die like carrion being eaten by a pack of scavengers. He and Bonnie had survived a quetzalcoatl, a storm flier, a whole herd of unicorns, a whole pack of feral hawk wyverns, a flock of cherubim, a cluster of rock drakes. Hell, Guy had survived the damn Tribulation. And he was going to die here because a stupid building collapsed and nearly crushed them, leaving him vulnerable to the stupid little critters running around on the ground he never thought he'd have to worry about.

Guy screamed as the pack pulled him out from under Bonnie, finally wrenching his broken leg free. He flailed as much as he could, but there were at least five of them taking turns nipping at him.

The armor of his riding suit and his helmet had protected him from the worst of the hurt from the fall. It was all made with Wellspring material and therefore could only be damaged by other things made from Wellspring material, which unfortunately included the teeth and claws of the predators now savaging him. The fabric that had been indestructible under concrete and rebar tore under their talons, drawing blood and more screams from him. Realistically his only chance at survival would have been his WS rifle, but he'd used up his bullet ration trying to keep Bonnie alive in the fight, so the weapon hung empty on Bonnie's saddle.

He reached down to his belt and pulled out the Bowie knife sheathed there. It was also made of Wellspring material and therefore could hurt the raptors if he managed to land a hit before one of them clamped onto his arm, which he didn't. He dropped the knife and screamed as the beast's teeth pierced his armor, pulling his arm like it meant to pull it off.

He thought his comm wasn't working anymore based on the static it was transmitting instead of voices, but on the off chance his mic was still hot, whoever was listening must be getting an earful.

Bonnie let out a whine and flopped her wings, trying to muster up the strength to push off the debris pinning her. The raptors finally managed to snap the lines keeping him attached to Bonnie's saddle, which whipped back with a *twang*. Now that he was completely untethered, the largest raptor clamped his torso in its jaws and ran off, his legs dragging across the dusty ground. The others followed, growling and jostling to try and take Guy from the pack leader.

"Bonnie!" he screamed, because for some reason the thought of dying away from her was *so* much less bearable.

Bonnie lay her head down limply, braying and moaning.

One of the raptors managed to get its jaws around his helmet and pull hard enough to rip it off. His hair came free. One of them seemed to find that interesting, nibbling at it and then getting a mouthful and tugging, taking out the cord he'd used to tie it back.

He hit the dirt with a *thud*, under the claws of one of the raptors, the others still squabbling over him. Multiple jaws and claws tugged him in different directions.

The rest of their force could be seen retreating overhead, the sky darkening intermittently with shadows of fleeing dragons. It felt odd, quiet, to not be able to hear the constant radio chatter that always accompanied being in an attack.

He tried to crane his neck to catch sight of Bonnie, but he'd been dragged too far away. He was alone. He hoped Bonnie could make it back on her own.

The pain was so intense he could hardly feel it anymore. His body was shutting down. He was so tired. Maybe this wasn't so bad. Maybe he shouldn't fight anymore. He let his limbs fall limp.

He closed his eyes and waited for it to happen.

Suddenly there was a huge stomping sound and the ground shook. The raptors gave alarm calls to each other and turned their attention towards something out of view, hissing and posturing. Then they fled entirely, leaving him completely exposed and limp on the pavement. Alone.

At first he thought Bonnie had managed to get up and come to save him. He weakly dragged his head across the ground to face the direction the raptors had fled from.

Oh, there was a new beast there. Big. Bigger than Bonnie herself. It stood on its hind legs and balanced with a heavy tail, and rows of curving spikes branched from its head down its back. It had a solid jaw like a saw, in which one of the raptors was currently hanging limply.

It dropped onto all fours and let the dead raptor fall to the pavement, then sniffed it, licked its lips, and started eating it. It used the massive claws on its forelegs to tear it apart.

Ah. He'd just be prey for a different predator, then. He let his head fall back down, trying to regulate his breathing. His mind swam in the pain, making it hard to think.

He watched the beast eat its meal, bones and all, cracking it apart into pieces and swallowing it without chewing, just tilting its head back and letting it slide down its throat. Like an alligator. Those were extinct now too.

The raptors came back in a nervous wave, picking their way towards Guy slowly in the hopes of not drawing the ire of the larger predator. Its eyes burned on them, and it trundled over towards Guy and shooed them away, dragging the bloody corpse of its half-eaten meal behind it. The raptors darted towards him in turns, rebuffed by the occasional claw or snarl from the beast claiming him as its meal.

He closed his eyes and just listened to the sounds. The squeaks, barks, thumping growls he could feel in his chest. A clawed foot pressed down on him from above, just barely not crushing him any more than he already was.

He bit his lip to keep from crying out. He was so tired. He lay there limply.

He felt hot breath on the back of his neck, a stinky exhale that disturbed his hair. He started to tremble, then, despite himself. This was it.

He cracked an eye open and saw the bloody muzzle of the big beast inches away from him, nostrils flaring to sniff him. Bits of the dead raptor were scattered about, a few stray bones and sinews still hanging from its teeth. The raptors were all gone, so the beast must have completed the first course of its meal and was now ready to eat him. This was it.

He squeezed his eyes shut again and turned away.

Its thick, coarse lips brushed against his skin, painting him with warm blood. He shuddered on the ground, still pinned under its broad claw. It nosed at him with something akin to curiosity, and it started to nibble on him. He let out a pathetic cry as its teeth scraped his skin, drawing even more blood. His head spun.

It drew back. He opened his eyes and looked up at it, chest heaving with terrified breaths. Its eyes were dark and inscrutable, but it was *looking* at him. Making eye contact.

"H ... hello?" he said. "Hi. I'm just some guy. Eyyyyyy."

Its jaw hinged all the way open, then, and clamped around him, adding even more punctures to his already impressive collection. He screamed and squirmed as it hefted him up in the air. It was so big he fit in its mouth sideways from shoulders to knees, only one arm left dangling outside of its mouth.

"Not a fan of jokes, then?" he managed to choke out before the shifting of its jaws drew out another terrified squeak.

The crushing force that he'd expected to come down and kill him didn't come, though. Instead the beast started walking. He swayed in its jaws, its teeth prickling him with the shambling motion. Carrying him away.

2

Guy expected the beast was taking him back to its nest to feed its young. There was no other explanation for why it would kidnap him, rather than just eating him on the spot. It was what Wellspring creatures did. They killed and ate and raised young and did basically nothing else.

It took him into one of the skyscrapers, one of the ones leaning precipitously into its neighbor. A huge hole had been blown in the side, and the creature picked its way across the wreckage carefully.

It crossed what would have once been a lobby, blue marble cracked and plants growing up through it and smothering the reception desk. It walked past what would have once been an elevator and mounted what remained of the stairs.

It barely fit in the stairwell, having to go partially up onto the wall to navigate the corners. A few times, it leapt over spaces where the stairs had collapsed entirely. It was a smart place to build a nest. Larger predators wouldn't be able to fit in the space, and smaller ones wouldn't be able to get over the obstacles or wouldn't be smart enough to climb the stairs at all.

The beast pushed past a broken door to exit the stairwell and come out onto a floor that looked like it had once been an office. The cubicles had all been pushed into one corner and piled up to form a sort of little shelter, facing away from the broken windows that would let in rain. Leaves and unidentifiable fabric and bones and dried blood lined the nest. Guy would almost call it cozy, even if it smelled terrible.

There were no young in the nest. No egg. Nothing at all. Guy's mind swam through the upstream of terror to try and make sense of it.

The creature gently set him onto the ground in the nest, then curled around him and put its head on its paws.

Guy swallowed, sweating. This ... wasn't what he'd expected. He palmed the floor to try and push himself to his feet, but the creature let out a savage growl and narrowed its eyes at him, nostrils flaring. He fell still immediately.

The beast's breathing gradually began to slow down, and when he looked over and saw its eyes sliding closed, he realized it was falling asleep. He waited a few minutes before once again trying to stand up, but it immediately snapped awake and growled at him again, even angrier than before. He froze, quaking.

He lost track of how long he lay there. The light outside started to dim as the sun set. Despite the whole situation, he was tired too. He was bone-deep exhausted. Despite the pain, he eventually fell asleep too.

***

It was still dark when he jolted awake, scrambling to remember where he was and what had happened.

The beast was gone. His heart pounded at the realization. It was gone, and everything was quiet, and *goddamn* did his everything still hurt, but he had to do something.

He had to get back down to the street, navigate the terrain through the dark, dodge hungry Wellspring creatures, find Bonnie, and get back to Wasp Nest.

... There was no way he could do that, not really. But he had to try, right?

Gritting his teeth to keep from crying out, he pushed himself to his feet, using a nearby desk to steady himself. *Okay. So far so good.*

He hobbled across the room. This was harder than he'd thought. He needed something to use as a crutch. Anything that could prop himself up.

There was a bent stop sign on the ground nearby. Sure. Why not. He bent down painfully to pick it up, then used it to brace himself and keep the pressure off his leg.

He made it to the stairwell okay. It was an agonizing pace, but he took the steps one at a time, wheezing.

It'd been a while since he'd been in a building this tall. It was giving him flashbacks to the before times. His father taking him to work in a building like this. Lots of paper and electronic devices and men in suits looking important.

He came to a section of the stairwell where the stairs had crumbled away. Ah. He'd forgotten. It was too far to jump, but there was still a bit of a lip attached to the wall. Maybe he could shimmy across it?

He put his good leg onto the ledge, and it crumbled instantly and tumbled down into the darkness below, sending him scrambling back.

Okay, so that wouldn't work. Maybe he could find something to lay across it, or a rope to swing across?

As he was in the process of assessing the surrounding rubble for anything useful, he heard the shuffling motions of the beast coming back upstairs.

Shit, oh shit shit shit shit. He froze with panic, having no idea what to do.

The beast's head appeared around the corner, and its eyes landed on him. It flicked an ear.

"Um," he said. "Hi."

It snorted and crouched down like it was going to jump. Guy scrambled backwards to get out of the landing zone, and when it leapt up, its claws slammed down a few inches in front of him.

It took a step forward, over him. He scrunched himself down, trying to become one with the concrete. "Hi," he said, voice getting even more mousey. "Um. Sorry."

He let out a scared *eep* as its mouth closed around him again, teeth prickling at him. He went limp in its jaws.

It carted him back up to the office nest and dropped him back where he'd been. He curled up in the corner, wrapping his arms around his legs. "Can't blame a guy for trying."

It made eye contact with him.

"A guy? Because I'm ... "

The beast turned away and walked back down the stairs.

Guy craned his neck to try and follow its motion, but its tail disappeared down into the dark. "Okay. Um, bye."

It came back up a moment later, this time with another dead raptor in its jaws. The corpse swung limply as the beast trotted over.

To his dismay, the beast leaned over and dropped the carcass directly onto Guy's lap.

He winced and squirmed, blood dripping down over his lap. "Um."

The beast lowered its head and sniffed at the corpse.

"Um." He held his hands up and leaned away, awash in discomfort and terror.

The beast bumped the corpse with its nose, pushing it towards him.

It suddenly clicked. "Are you ... are you trying to feed me?"

The beast sat back on its haunches, tail swishing.

Guy looked from the carcass to the beast and back again, utterly amazed. "Thank you, but. Um ... I can't eat this. I'm not sure what you want me to do."

It gave a bovine low and shook its head, ears flicking.

"Um, I'm sorry. Don't, uh, don't be mad at me."

It tugged the corpse off his lap and dragged it away, tearing it open and starting to eat it. Guy let himself relax a little, trying to wipe the blood from himself. Between the blood and the smell in here and the sweat and tears and everything from earlier, Guy felt *disgusting* in a way that would be intolerable if the fear of his imminent demise wasn't so looming.

Although ... given the way the thing was behaving, maybe it wasn't so imminent after all.

3

Guy watched the beast for a bit, studying it. It was behaving ... strangely for a Wellspring creature. He'd never encountered one that didn't just try to eat him as soon as it clapped eyes on him. It seemed smarter. More on the level of the hawk wyverns the guild members rode, which could be cooperative and trained, the only Wellspring creatures capable of that kind of behavior. Except for this one, apparently. The beast seemed relatively normal other than that, cracking the bones of its prey and swallowing it down in an animalistic way.

Guy stretched his legs out, the injury in his left leg twinging with pain now that the adrenaline had worn off. The beast was currently facing away from him, and it seemed inappropriate to do so, but he examined the space between its hind legs. There was no evidence of maleness there, so it was probably female, although Wellspring creatures could get pretty freaky about that sometimes. Guy had spent his fair share of time in the library at Paramount reading up on the cataloged information on Well springs and the phenomenon associated with them. Everyone was required to do so as part of their training to become a dragonrider, but he'd been among the few to take it seriously. The younger trainees just kind of blew it off, in his experience.

So the beast was a girl beast. "Beast?" he said.

She raised her head and looked at him, blood dribbling from her maw.

"Can I name you Bea?"

She flicked an ear and lowered her head, going back to her meal.

Guy felt silly. A Wellspring creature could not possibly care less what you called it, but for some reason it felt like he needed to name it. If she was a *she* and *Bea* and a familiar beast, that was less scary. As though he could will it into existence that this creature could be won over, just like he'd won Bonnie over.

Guy shakily got to his feet, steadying himself on the nearby furniture. "Hey, Bea?"

Bea ignored him this time, unwavering attention on finishing her meal.

Guy limped closer. "Were you really trying to feed me?"

The last of the raptor finally disappeared down her throat, and she licked her chops, sniffing the ground to make sure it was really all gone.

"Why are you keeping me here?"

Her eyes swung towards him. He really could not tell what was going on behind them – if there was any intelligence there. It felt like there was, but maybe he was imagining it.

"I appreciate it," he said. "I do. I can't eat Wellspring creatures, though. It's just – "

She abruptly got up and disappeared down the stairwell, snorting and flicking her tail dismissively.

" ... Okay," he said quietly.

***

Guy spent the alone time imagining what would happen if he did eat the meat of a Wellspring creature. His stomach acid couldn't break down the meat any more than his punch could hurt its body while it was still alive. Very best-case scenario, he'd throw it back up. Though it'd probably just sit in his gut like he'd eaten a piece of metal.

He thought better about trying to go down the stairs this time. He doubted he could make it all the way down to the ground floor, and even if he did, his reward would be facing whatever creatures were down there. Not as puzzlingly inclined to nonviolence towards him as Bea, but surely just as hungry.

He limped over to one of the broken windows, leaning on it and looking outside. He watched the sunrise with a strange sense of inner peace. Everything felt like it mattered less, here, his world shrunk down to whether or not Bea was going to eat him in this nest.

A pack of fox wyverns flew by outside in the distance, the *pop* of their teleportation powers echoing off the buildings. Guy gasped and dropped down, below the window. He'd managed to forget for a moment where he was. The kind of danger he was perpetually in.

He sighed and looked around the room. In his haste to make an escape, he hadn't picked over the debris of this floor very much. It had been an open office concept of some sort, he guessed, because it seemed like most of the floor was one giant room.

His stomach growled. He really was starting to get hungry. He hadn't eaten since breakfast yesterday, before leaving Wasp Nest to join the battle against the horde of creatures that had been menacing the farming settlement across the river.

He found a rusty metal pipe this time to use as a crutch, balancing on it as he hobbled around broken desks and chairs and moldy cubicles and bits of rubble from the collapsed upper floor. He poked around for anything useful.

A dirt-filled pot, some houseplant long dead and gone. Trinkets and doodads people had used to decorate their desks, brightly-colored plastic figures lying faded and broken on the floor. Paper, ever-present paper, yellowed and tattered and molding. Electronic devices that hadn't worked in decades – broken touchscreens, ripped power cords, hardware snapped in half. Conference rooms with the glass barriers smashed out. A water cooler, the interior long bone-dry. A bathroom, the toilet in an unspeakable state. He tried the faucet just to check – a rusty sludge came out. It would probably be more dangerous to drink than puddle water from outside. He left it on just in case it eventually started running clear water.

At last, something useful: a vending machine. It was still upright and fully stocked. He tried pressing the buttons first – they didn't work, of course, without power. But worth a shot. Next he tried jamming his arm up in through the dispensing port to grab whatever was on the lowest shelf. No chance. He resigned himself to having to pick glass out of whatever he grabbed and smashed the front with the metal pipe.

The dirty glass cascaded down, giving him a clear view of the contents inside. Some of the snacks had clearly rotted and started growing mold even through their sealed packaging, but some of them looked like they might be okay. He reached in and took one, shaking it to get all the glass off, and tore it open. It was some sort of chocolate pastry, desiccated and discolored. It smelled off, so he tossed it to the ground and reached for the thing beside it. The label printed on the side indicated it had expired in 2067. He shrugged and tore it open. He took a nibble despite his better judgment, then immediately spat it out.

He sighed and reached for one of the cans of soda. This one had no expiration date, and when he cracked it open, it still fizzled. Of course. These kinds of manmade liquid abominations lasted forever.

He took a sip. It was ... *incredibly* sweet. He didn't entirely like it. Had he really eaten and drunk things like this every day before the Tribulation?

It wasn't filling in the slightest, but it did give him some much needed energy. He continued rifling around to find anything useful until Bea came back.

He heard her before he saw her, big stomps up the stairs. He came over to meet her. "Hey, girl! Did you have a good day at work?"

She flicked her tail and narrowed her eyes at him. She approached and lowered her head.

Guy took a nervous step back.

She opened her mouth, and a handful of dented cans tumbled out, rolling across the floor.

Guy stared at them in amazement. Canned pineapples, potatoes, and pumpkin puree. That's what they were.

"Oh my God. You *are* trying to feed me." He got down on his knees and collected the cans, trying to calculate how best to take advantage of this strange blessing. "Thank you. Um. Thanks."

She sat down, curling her tail around her front feet. Guy kept the cans in his arms and walked with some difficulty over towards a pile of debris he'd seen earlier, where a twisted metal bar had a jagged edge he'd noted he'd need to avoid.

He held the can up to it and twisted, using it as a can opener. Pineapple juice spilled out.

"Thank you, Bea," he said. "Thank you. Holy shit." He sipped at the juice – it tasted funny after drinking the soda. He reached a dirty finger in and scooped up a pineapple ring. A *pineapple ring.* He hadn't eaten pineapple since before the Tribulation.

It was sweet and acidic in his mouth. He couldn't stifle the little moan of satisfaction. "Bea, you're beautiful. You're a gem."

She stalked over to where he was, watching him. He made eye contact with her, trying to make it obvious that he was making use of what she'd brought back, eating it with exaggerated glee.

"We used to make a really good kind of cake with these, you know," he said wistfully. "With brown sugar. You'd bake a cake using pineapple juice instead of water, then turn it upside down at the end. The glaze would all dribble down." He sat down, hunched over. He was imagining the pineapple upside-down cake so vividly he could almost taste it.

He sighed and took another bite of pineapple ring. "The rest of my unit wouldn't have even known about that kind of cake. I wonder if any of them ever even ate pineapple. They were all so young."

Bea sat down, ear twitching.

"They were just kids, Bea. My God, they were just kids. They didn't even understand the difference between the magic of the Wellsprings and the technology of, like, the mics in our helmets and stuff. They thought Awsk was a person and not an AI. They didn't even know what an AI *was.*"

But he hadn't gotten attached to them, so it was fine. He hadn't gotten attached to anyone since his first unit. He'd learned. "I knew they weren't going to last, Bea. They were stupid and reckless. Too eager to fight. Too excited about the thought of dying in battle." When had he started crying? He reached a sticky hand up and wiped the tears on the back of his palm. "They never last. Even the kids. Especially the kids."

He startled as Bea shoved her snout under his hand. After a moment, he slowly lowered his hand down onto her, touching gently. "Thank you," he said around the lump in his throat. "God, I'm going to have to drink something other than Pepsi to stay hydrated if I'm going to be crying, huh? Haha."

***

Bea ended up bringing back an entire refrigerator the next time she left, the old, dirty appliance dragging on the ground in her jaws as she excitedly brought it back like a retriever. It was completely empty, but she seemed to know it was associated with food somehow, because she dropped it at his feet the same way she'd done with the cans earlier.

"Thank you," he said very seriously. He opened it and put the remaining canned food and soda in it, despite the fact that it was sitting on its side and unpowered. It did give him some weird feeling of normalcy. *Food goes in the fridge.*

He managed to collect some water when it rained that afternoon. He left some of the drums from the empty water cooler by the broken windows and torn-away walls, and they managed to catch some of the rainwater.

With imminent death staved off – relative safety, and starvation and dehydration kept at bay – he was now free to be incredibly in pain. His leg was very, very broken, and he still had multiple open wounds from the raptor attack – not actively bleeding, but threatening to reopen if they didn't get some proper treatment soon. He couldn't afford to pass out from blood loss.

Fuck it. If he was going to be stuck here with this beast of unknown intentions, he might as well try. "Hey, Bea?" he said tentatively.

She raised her head off her paws.

"I need some medicine." She seemed capable of understanding more than expected. Could she understand that? Would this unexpected blessing stretch that far? "I'm hurt. I'm sick."

She got up, stretched, and came over to him, shoving her snout in his face. He scrambled backwards. "Medicine?" he said hopefully.

She nosed at him. A pit formed in his stomach. Had he made a mistake?

Her jaws opened and clamped around him, lifting him bodily up. *Oh fuck.* Yep, yep, yep, definitely a mistake. Somehow.

25

"Wait, Bea!" he cried, squirming in her jaws. Her iron-hard teeth prickled at him. "Wait, I'm sorry. I'm sorry."

She ignored his thrashing around and carried him down the stairs, effortlessly leaping over the gulfs that had given him trouble. They came out onto the ground floor, and Bea galloped over the uneven pavement, still keeping him clamped in her jaws.

A large shadow passed overhead, the outline of a predator far larger than Bea herself. She huddled under an overturned bus until it passed, then continued on with her mission.

"Where are we going?" Guy asked, trying not to sound too pitiful.

She grunted, and Guy felt the vibrations in his core. All she'd need to do would be to clamp down and break him in half, and that would be it for him.

She didn't, though. She toted him through the ruined streets and passed through a few tunnels, coming out into –

The world tumbled over as Bea dropped Guy onto the linoleum. He rolled over, groaning, and froze when his foot touched something.

A box. Bandages. *A box of bandages.*

"Holy shit," he said, nearly weeping with relief. He looked around and saw the destroyed remains of a pharmacy. "Holy shit. You're a lifesaver. Thank you, thank you."

He crawled along the floor, collecting bandages and ointments and bottles of pills. "Holy shit. Bea, I don't know what the hell you are or why you're doing this, but thank you. You're a lifesaver."

He managed to find a case of bottled water, then turned a chair over so he could sit on it. He stripped his shirt off and started pouring the water over his open wounds. He brushed the dirt off a bar of soap he'd found and used it to clean out the many, many bite marks littering his skin as best as he could. He found a rubber band to tie his hair back and keep it out of his face.

He applied the antibiotic ointment and wrapped his bites up in the bandages. He then wiggled out of his pants to repeat the procedure for the wounds on his legs.

Bea snorted, lying down on her haunches and tail wiggling.

Guy froze, self-consciousness suddenly creeping over him. "Don't look at me like that."

Bea had an amused glint in her eye, and she snorted.

"Don't objectify me!"

She crawled forwards and hooked his pants with one claw, dragging them away.

"Hey! You little pervert!"

He finished washing out the cuts on his legs and wrapping them up, feeling woozy from all the blood he'd lost in the past twenty-four hours. There was probably more Pepsi and pineapple juice than blood in his veins at this point.

He pulled his top back on, bandages now showing through the holes, and reached towards his pants. Bea had them in her mouth.

"Please?" he said, trying not to sound too desperate.

She snorted and tossed her head. The pants landed on Guy's face.

"Thank you." He stepped back into them, trying mightily not to jostle his broken leg. The very expired acetaminophen he'd swallowed earlier could only do so much.

He hunted around and found a boot and a splint, which he used to immobilize the leg, as well as a very high tech first aid kit. There was a syringe inside that the leaflet instructed him to use in the event of broken bones. He never knew what was in those things, but he'd been told they worked.

He tried to confirm the needle wasn't too dirty before stabbing it into his leg. As soon as he injected it, pain ripped like wildfire through the area, and he fell down squirming.

"Jesus Christ," he moaned, rolling over. "Fuuuuck me. This is it. This is how I die."

The pain passed after a minute, and his hazy vision cleared to see Bea standing over him and nosing him with concern.

"I'm all right." He heaved in big breaths and used her head to help stand up, using the horns as handholds. "Shit. Fuck." His leg *did* feel a bit better now, but that might just be compared to how it'd felt when the injection hit.

He found an honest-to-goodness crutch nearby, and with that, it was really all he could ask for for a broken leg right now. He hunted around and found a backpack lying open on the ground – it'd belonged to some ill-fated scavengers, no doubt. He hung it on his front and loaded the remaining bottled water into it. He'd need it to stay hydrated if he had diarrhea later, which he suspected was coming from all the very expired food he was eating.

He collected the rest of the bandages, pain meds, first aid kit, and whatever else he could find that seemed useful and stowed it in the backpack, limping along with his crutch.

All things considered, this was good. Very good. Maybe he *wasn't* going to die. Maybe he could survive, somehow. Maybe he could …

Maybe he could find Bonnie.

Bea clearly had some level of irregular intelligence and some inclination to use it to help him. He didn't want to push his luck, especially since he couldn't guarantee how Bonnie would react to Bea, but *damn* did he want to go find her. The longer he waited, the less chance there was of finding her alive.

"Hey, Bea," he said slowly. He walked towards the thumping of her big feet. "So, I was wondering. Can you – "

He stopped as he rounded the bend and saw that the thing that had been stomping around was *not* Bea. It had a tail, which was a writhing snake, pointing at him. As soon as its slitted eyes clamped onto him, the second head at the front, which was a lion, looked over its shoulder at him.

Chimera. "Fuck," Guy said, scrambling backwards and stumbling into an overturned store shelf.

The chimera backed up to get him within range of its tail, and the snake lashed out and bit him.

"Fuck," he said again, and he smacked the snake head with his crutch. It did nothing, of course. He had nothing that could hurt it, not his knife or his gun or his dragon.

He did have Bea, though. She barreled around the corner and pounced on the chimera's head, cracking its skull with her enormous weight. The lion claws came out and sunk into her feet, and the wings flapped and the tail writhed.

Bea closed her mouth around its head and crushed it. It fell still, the tail still wiggling directionlessly.

"Thanks, Bee," he said. He started to sweat. "I really thought – I didn't know if – you were – were ... gonna ... "

The strength bled out of his limbs. *Oh no*, he thought, skin crawling. *No, no, I'm fucked. I'm so fucked.*

The chimera's paralyzing venom kicked in fully, sapping his ability to speak and stand. His knees collapsed from under him and he went down.

All he could move were his eyes, which bounced around at floor-level. He felt the floor vibrate with shaking footsteps. Bea, for real this time, he hoped.

Tears streamed down his face and onto the floor. *Fuck.* No way Bea would be able to keep him alive like this, right? He had no idea how long it was going to take the venom to wear off, and that was assuming he hadn't been given a fatal dose. He tried to move, something, *anything*, even to twitch his fingers, but all he could do was gulp in panicked breaths and look around.

Bea's snout came into his field of view, snuffling over him.

"Bea," he managed to get out.

She nosed at him, pushing him over onto his back. His head lolled.

"Bea," he faintly said again.

Her teeth closed around him, and as she carted him off this time, he wasn't even worried about where they were going.

4

To add insult to injury, the venom had forcibly relaxed *all* his muscles, including his bowels, and his earlier predictions about his bodily functions came true. So now he had to sit in that.

He was limp like a doll in Bea's jaws, swinging like the corpse she'd brought in earlier. He wondered if Bea would mistake him for dead and finally eat him, although maybe she would be too grossed out by him shitting his pants to do that.

She dropped him in her nest like she always had, and this time he just lay there where he'd been dropped, overwhelmed tears prickling at his eyes again.

She nosed at him, rolling him over.

"Bea," he gasped weakly. "Please."

She snorted and nosed at him again, as though urging him to get up.

"I can't. I can't move."

She circled around behind him and hooked her teeth in his shirt, dragging him back and leaning him against the wall of the nest. That was better than lying on the floor, at least, even if his head lay limply on the furniture next to him.

***

Bea circled him relentlessly, occasionally nosing at him to get up. When she eventually got bored of that, she lay down and curled up around him again.

When all was quiet outside, he fell asleep despite being terrified he might not wake back up.

He did, though. Bea had laid out on her back, belly up in the air.

His mouth was so, so dry. "Bea? I'm so thirsty. Can you get me water?"

She rolled over, ears flopping, and looked at him.

"Water?" He would have pantomimed drinking something to give her the idea, but he still couldn't move.

She rose to her feet and stuck her snout into the backpack that was still dangling from his chest. She came back out with a bottle of water delicately clenched between her teeth.

"Yes," he said, relief flooding through him. "Yes, yes, water. Thank you."

She let it fall onto his lap. He groaned, trying not to cry and become even more dehydrated. "I can't move, Bea. Please. I need help. Please hclp."

She nosed at the bottle of water.

"I need help."

She delicately clenched the bottle again, raising it up to his face.

"You need to open it."

Her teeth punctured it, and the water all drained and fell onto his lap. He tried not to let out a hopeless whimper, but it happened anyway.

Growling with frustration, Bea went into the backpack again and came out with another bottle of water. This one she gripped in her claws, but it was obvious she didn't have the manual dexterity needed to open it that way. She pawed at it like a dog, and eventually this one crumpled and burst under her claws too.

Guy tried to stifle his sounds of despair. Bea growled and shook her head, crinkling the water bottle and ripping it up.

"Bee," he said desperately. "Please. I'm going to die here. I'm going to die if you can't help me."

Bea paced back and forth, swinging her head and chuffing to herself. Then she stopped and turned around, nosing open the fridge and clamping one of the cans in her mouth.

She held it in her mouth and turned it over and over until her top fang pierced the lid of the can. The juice inside welled up.

Guy was so thirsty it almost hurt to look at. "Please."

With as much dexterity as she could muster, Bea positioned herself above Guy and tilted the can so the juice dribbled down.

Wonder of wonders, she managed to get a decent amount in his mouth.

***

Bea repeated this strategy with the cans of potatoes, and Guy never thought stinky potato water would taste so good. The pumpkin puree was a bit of a mess – it sloshed down all over him, adding to the mess, but it kept him alive through the day, then the night, then the next day, until –

He managed to twitch a finger. He sobbed with relief, then. By that afternoon he was able to reach down and grab a water bottle for himself, twist it open, and take sips.

"Thank you, Bea," he said. She drew near, lowering her snout so he could pat it weakly. "You've saved my life yet again."

She let out a rumble.

Guy took a few hours to get back on his feet and although it was wobbly, he could walk around now. He collapsed back into the nest at nightfall, exhausted once again and ready for a good night's sleep.

5

— ◦ —

He was feeling almost normal the next morning. Even his leg was hurting less – apparently the emergency bone juice he'd shot into himself was helping, or maybe it was just the boot. Bea hadn't taken the crutch he'd found at the pharmacy, but he couldn't really blame her for that and resorted to once again finding a metal pipe and propping himself up.

He ate the last of the canned food – dry, raw potatoes weren't his idea of the breakfast of champions, but it was what they had. "Hey, Bee. I'm filthy. Do you think we could find running water somewhere for me to wash off and change my bandages? We're going to need more food soon too, maybe we can look for that while we're out?"

She grunted her assent and then seized him once again in her mouth. He was going to have to figure out a way to ask her not to do that.

She carefully picked her way through the ruins again, sticking to cover to avoid the notice of predators that could fly or were bigger than her. She eventually prowled into what had clearly been a public park at one point, the trails long overgrown and the benches and playgrounds sitting in disrepair.

Trees crowded in on the path and blocked it from overhead view, and the shade felt nice. Bea approached a drop-off and slid down it through the dried leaves and underbrush, sliding to a stop at a creek bed.

She dropped him on the edge, and he dipped a finger in. "Oh, this is lovely. This is such a nice spot." He raised his head and closed his eyes, feeling the dappled sunlight on his skin and remembering what birdsong had sounded like in a place like this. Forests were quiet these days. He hadn't seen a wild bird in years, and even insects were typically in short supply as the smaller Wellspring creatures had devastated their populations.

The plants were abundant, though. Wellspring creatures were all carnivores.

Guy waded into the creek and found it a pleasant temperature, cool but not too cold, having been warmed by the sun. It went up to about his waist. Relieved to finally have some reasonable way to wash himself, he stripped his shirt, then his pants. He washed them off as best as he could, then lay them out flat on a nearby rock to dry.

He unwrapped his bandages and let them flow away in the stream. He dipped his wounds in the water carefully – he wasn't sure the water was clean, but surely anything would be better than not cleaning out the filth he'd been sitting in for the past few days. Luckily the antibiotic ointment seemed to be pulling its weight and all his injuries were scabbed over with little inflammation.

He bent down and dipped his upper half in the water, scrubbing his hair out and dislodging the last of the nasty layer that had accumulated all over him. He waded back to shore and knelt to dig in his backpack to retrieve the bar of soap he had.

Bea was looking directly at his exposed genitals.

Guy froze, cheeks heating up. Should he be embarrassed by this? Should Bea be embarrassed? Was she capable of feeling embarrassed?

"Like what you see?" It was all he could think to say.

She flicked an ear and looked away. Guy scrutinized her very hard, trying to figure out what exactly was going on in her head.

He shrugged and retrieved the soap, wading back into the water. Bea continued to watch him as he scrubbed himself clean, looking extremely interested.

"Do you want to get clean too?" he asked carefully. Maybe if she washed off, everything in the nest would smell less horrible.

She tilted her head.

He made a motion like rubbing soap in the air. "I can clean you off."

Bea hauled herself to her feet and cautiously waded into the river after him. It barely came up past her knees.

"Go ahead and get nice and wet," Guy prompted.

She lowered herself down and rolled around in the creek, water splashing, sending a small tidal wave rolling over Guy.

"Hey!" he giggled. "Watch it!"

She rolled over, water dripping from her horns, watching him.

He playfully splashed her back. "How do *you* like it, huh?"

She let out a bray that sounded suspiciously like laughter, and a mighty swipe of her paw sent another huge swell of water crashing over him. He laughed and let himself float with it.

The water sloshed around her legs as she waded towards him. She peered over, toothy delight on her warped face.

He splashed her again.

She reached her paw out and pinned him under the water.

All playfulness immediately fled Guy's body, visceral panic overtaking him as he flailed his limbs and tried to yell for her to let him up. In his panic, he simply swallowed a mouthful of water.

Oh God, oh my God, oh my fucking God, she's going to drown me. She has the strength to drown me with one hand and I can't do anything about it and maybe she doesn't even realize she's drowning me but –

In reality it must have only been a few seconds, but it felt like minutes. She let him up, and he immediately coughed up the water he'd inhaled, flailing and backing away from her.

Her face shifted downwards into a frown. Guy scooted backwards and braced himself against the pebbles on shore, water dripping down from his hair.

"Don't hurt me," he tried. "S-sorry, I'm sorry."

Bea looked *heartbroken*. He'd never seen any Wellspring creature emote, let alone with such clarity. It was even clearer than
the body language of the hawk wyverns he was used to.

Guy coughed again. "Um. It's – "

Fear surged through him again as Bea's snout drew closer, but
she merely rested it in his lap. A mournful rumble vibrated her
throat.

Guy's hand slowly lowered down to stroke her head.

"It was just an accident. You just scared me a little. I'm not
hurt."

Her eyes flickered up to him.

"We just gotta be a bit more careful when we're goofing
around, I guess."

She closed her eyes.

"Now come on, let me up so I can put fresh bandages on."

Still looking downtrodden, she removed herself from him
and stayed low to the ground. He rifled in his backpack to find
the bandages and ointment, wrapping himself up liberally. His
clothes were still pretty damp, but he didn't want to wait here
too long for them to dry, so he stretched the wet fabric of his
suit over his shoulders and put it back on. He then replaced the
boot on his leg.

"Hey, Bee, I need your help with something. Will you help
me a little more?"

She raised her head.

"My best friend is named Bonnie. She's a lot like you. She's still out there, hurt and scared. Will you help me find her?"

She got to her feet and made a motion to clamp him in her jaws. "Ah-hah," he said, sweating. "Could we maybe, um, do that some other way? Your teeth hurt me."

Bea lowered her head and moaned mournfully.

"It's okay! I promise it's okay. You just didn't realize. What about if I sit up on your back?"

Bea looked over her shoulder, then slowly lowered down.

Guy used her spiked horns as handholds, navigating carefully to sit down on her shoulders. Okay, this wasn't so different from a dragon. He would have to use more upper body strength than core this way, but he felt much safer up here in the familiar territory of riding a huge beast.

Except Bea didn't have a saddle and reins, and also hadn't been trained to understand the cues with his boots. He went to dig his heels into her flank out of muscle memory before remembering she'd have no idea what that meant.

"Um, okay," he said instead. "Do you remember where you found me? Can you take me back there?"

Bea moved off. Okay, this wasn't too different. Hawk wyverns usually took verbal commands pretty well – they were wicked smart, relatively speaking, and understood what you were telling them sometimes. They couldn't hear you well during flight, though, hence the need for nonverbal cues.

41

Hawk wyverns were the only Wellspring creature who could understand spoken speech, as far as he knew. Just another reason why Bea was unusual.

Bea meandered around a while as though she couldn't quite remember the way, but eventually she corrected herself and made a beeline for the site where he and Bonnie had fallen.

His heart sank. Bonnie wasn't where he'd last seen her. The debris lay scattered over empty concrete. That was good, he told himself. As long as he hadn't seen her body, there was a chance she was still alive.

He asked Bea to let him off and he rummaged around until he found his Bowie knife. He sheathed it, pleased to no longer be *completely* helpless. His helmet was nearby, scraped and banged up but still perfectly functional. Good, he'd need it for when he found Bonnie. "Can we look around a little for her?"

He got back up on Bea's back, and they walked around, still sticking to cover to avoid notice. Guy wanted to call out for Bonnie like a lost cat; she'd come running if she heard his voice, but probably so would the other million monsters infesting the ruins.

Just as they were crossing from a bridge to a tunnel, Guy heard the distinct and in this case *terrifying* sound of a fox wyvern teleporting, *terrifyingly* close.

Talons closed around his shoulders, yanking him off Bea's back, too fast for him to react. His suit protected him from the worst of the claws, but it wouldn't save him from –

There was another *pop* of teleportation, and suddenly he was a million miles off the ground. And in free fall a second later when his assailant released him.

"Oh God!" he screamed, tumbling head over heels. "Bonnie! Bonnie! BONNIE BONNIE BONNIE!"

And wonder of wonders, Bonnie answered. Guy had been right about her coming running if he shouted for her.

She gave an alarm call and launched into flight from some unseen crevice where she'd been hiding, pumping her wings to get up into the air. He'd never seen her move so fast, not even to get treats. She looked incredibly disheveled but otherwise okay.

The fox wyvern snarled and maneuvered itself to intercept Bonnie. Clearly it intended to just follow him down and have its meal after the fall did the hard work of killing him – not a sophisticated strategy, but an effective one without another creature meddling.

He willed Bonnie to meddle faster.

Bonnie was quite a bit larger than the fox wyvern, and so she simply barreled straight through it, knocking it away in the air, completely ignoring its bites and claws raking over her in favor of getting to Guy as fast as possible. *That* was not a reaction a young rider would have gotten from their dragon, not until after years of bonding.

Her talons clamped around him, knocking the wind out of him as he was jerked sideways. Above him, Bonnie and the fox wyvern spiraled around clamped onto each other, snarling viciously.

But the fox wyvern was fighting for a meal and Bonnie was fighting for her human's life. Bonnie opened her mouth and exhaled a column of fire at the fox wyvern, and that was all it took for it to decide it wasn't worth the effort and fly off.

Bonnie alighted on a nearby rooftop, dropping Guy and chirping at him anxiously. He groaned and rolled over, pushing himself up. Her snout prodded at him, almost pushing him over. "I'm here, I'm here, girl."

He took her snout in his encircling arms and gave her a little kiss between her eyes. "Thank you so much. I missed you. I was so worried about you."

Bonnie let out deep, happy rumbles, tail thumping against the ground.

Okay, Bonnie's saddle was still here and usable even though the anchors had been snapped. He had his helmet and his riding suit. They were both banged up but in good enough shape to travel.

The logical next step was to just leave the city and head back to Wasp Nest. That was it. There really was no reason to hesitate and do anything else.

It would be stupid to not just immediately leave.

… It would be stupid.

Guy was realizing he was a little bit stupid.

"Hey, girl, I met somebody here who took care of me while we were separated. Do you want to go meet her?"

Bonnie looked at him and trilled nervously, hesitation written all over her features.

"She's like you. She's a big, um, a big, pointy gal. But she's nice. I was in a real bad spot and she made sure I didn't die. She's probably worried about me." Why the hell should he care if a Wellspring creature was "worried about him"? What on earth could that even mean?

... And yet the thought of Bea wandering around, anxiously looking for him in the rubble, was too much.

And Guy had never met any creature like Bea before. Maybe nobody had. It was extremely unusual. It could be important.

Bonnie did not seem convinced. Her tail twitched, feathers fanning out.

"She can't fly," Guy offered. "If she decides to attack, we can just fly away."

Bonnie hesitantly lowered her wing down so Guy could access her saddle and climb on.

It felt good to be back in the saddle, even if it was hard to settle in with his foot in a boot. The leg straps were still functional, so that should give him some security to not fall out of the saddle. Her reins were gone, but he could manage well enough without them for a while. Bonnie usually knew what to do.

Bonnie trotted over and climbed a building to get up high enough to throw herself into the air so they could start circling the city.

6

It was hard to find Bea. She knew to avoid being out in the open where aerial predators could take a swipe at her – the fact that a fox wyvern had managed to snatch him off her back had honestly been incredibly unlucky.

He spotted her tail disappearing underneath a ruined overpass. "There," he said, and knowing Bonnie probably couldn't hear him, gave Bonnie's left shoulder a series of rapid taps. Bonnie took this as instructions to dive left and descend.

Her feet thumped in the dirt for a few paces before she stopped and folded in her wings. Guy could just barely make out the glow of Bea's eyes in the shadows under the overpass.

"Bea," he said, waving to her. "Bea, I'm here! I'm okay! Are you okay?"

Bea warily crept out. Bonnie hopped backwards, fanning her wings out and hissing defensively. Bea responded by crouching low to the ground, all her spikes facing outwards, and baring her teeth.

"It's okay!" Guy shouted. "Sh! Sh! Girls, girls, it's all right!"
He slid off Bonnie's saddle, hobbling forwards a few steps,
trying not to imagine himself being ripped in half as the two
massive creatures did a tug-of-war. Ironic – being fought over
by two large women had once been a fantasy of his.

"This is Bea," Guy said. "She saved my life. See?" He very
cautiously reached a hand out to Bea, who slunk forwards   and
pushed her snout into his palm. "Bea, this is Bonnie. She's my
best friend."

Bonnie gradually smoothed out her feathers and folded in her
wings, cocking her head in a birdlike motion and lashing her tail.
She let out a curious chirp and stepped forward, head bobbing.

Bea gradually untensed, keeping low and sniffing. Bonnie
leaned in to do the same, and the two both jerked backwards as
they accidentally bumped each other.

"It's all right," Guy said with a laugh. "We're all friends here.
See?" He put his other hand on Bonnie's snout. "There we go.
See?"

Bea flattened herself against the ground, as though trying to
hide behind Guy.

"What is this?" he laughed. "Suddenly you're shy now?"

Bonnie's head snaked around and she very cautiously
touched her lips onto the furthest tip of one of Bea's spikes,
taking an exploratory nibble. Bea didn't seem bothered by it,
instead very curiously sniffing Bonnie's talons.

41

"Bee, here's the deal," Guy said. God, this was going to be ... something. "Bonnie and I have friends at the outpost south of here. We have to go back there. But I don't want to just leave you behind. Do you want to come with us?"

Bea slowly raised her head, ears flicking, eyebrows raising. She grunted.

"Yeah?"

She turned her head unsurely, bobbing and lowing.

"It'll be okay. I'll tell them what you did for me. They'll be able to see you're ... different. Not a threat. They'll take care of you, I know they will. They'll be so interested to learn everything about you." He pulled on Bonnie's saddle to reseat himself. "We should get going now so we can get there before sunset. What do you say?"

Bea shuffled along to follow as Guy gave Bonnie the command to move out.

***

He'd have to have Bea wait out of sight until he could get back to Wasp Nest and talk to General Hobby about it. Bea would be killed on sight unless everyone had been informed and told to hold off, even if they saw Bea approaching alongside Guy.

Bea seemed extremely unhappy now that the shoe was on the other foot and *she* had to trust *Guy*.

"I promise I'll come back. I *promise*. I just need you to stay here until I can tell everyone about you so they don't attack you. Okay?"

She gave an anxious moan and hunkered down.

Guy made sure she was hidden from the air before jetting off with Bonnie towards Wasp Nest. The sandy, limestone cliffs came into view, and there was the station itself perched atop. A massive building, half of which was the structure that gave Southern Station its nickname: the stables where the dragons nested was a lumpy structure twisting out from the building, with honeycomb-shaped nesting caverns.

Bonnie didn't need directions to climb to the top of the roost and swoop down in. Dragons, startled by the sudden appearance of an active dragon while the rest were trying to settle into their nests for the evening, flapped and barked at her.

"Is that Guy?" said the errant voice of a rider elsewhere in the room.

Bonnie found her preferred nest and landed, barely giving Guy enough time to dismount before flopping on her side and covering herself up with her wings.

"You did good," he said, patting her side. "Thank you. Make sure you get some dinner before you go to sleep."

"Lieutenant!" someone called. "We thought you were dead!"

Guy peered over the edge to see a loose group of other riders clustered on the ground, looking up at him.

"I told you you don't have to call me Lieutenant," Guy shouted back. "I'm really just some guy."

A chorus of groans came from below. "That's him, all right."

Guy swung around and started climbing down the ladder. "In the flesh."

"Where's the rest of Unit 24?"

"They didn't make it back, unless they showed up here while I was gone."

"Another unit wipe? Isn't this the third time? I'm starting to get suspicious."

"You got me. I'm a double agent. The Wellspring creatures are paying me to off my teammates." His boots hit the ground. "Where is the general? I need to talk to him right away."

***

The glowing lights from Sonny's giant computer screen shifted as he scrolled down. The screen had the words *ARCHIVE OF WELLSPRING KNOWLEDGE* at the top, and pictures of different Wellspring creatures flashed past.

"I'd say she's in the medium size category. She's bigger than Bonnie, but definitely smaller than Patches and Lucifer."

"Got it," said Awsk, and the images shifted once again, winnowing out all the ones that were too big or too small.

General Hobby thoughtfully stroked his beard. "Did she display any abilities we could use to narrow it down? What's the species' cheat?"

"I have no idea. I didn't see her breathe fire or teleport when either of those would be useful, so probably not that. Maybe her cheat is just being really smart?"

"Mmmm," Sonny said doubtfully.

"I haven't recorded anything like that yet," Awsk said, its disembodied voice just coming directly from the screen. "This sounds really unusual. You're sure this is correct?"

"Yes," Guy answered instantly. "I wouldn't be alive if it wasn't."

"This could potentially be something very important for the guild scientists to know," General Hobby said. "If we can confirm it."

"More spikes," Guy said. "None of these have enough spikes."

The images filtered further, until Guy saw a familiar one flash past. "There! There, that's what she looks like."

Awsk maximized the image.

"Damn, it looks a lot ... meaner than she does." It was bigger, had even more spikes, and perhaps most importantly not a hint or gleam of intelligence in its eyes. It looked like Bea's stupid older brother.

"It's called a porcupine, apparently," Awsk said. Guy could see that, maybe, if he'd never laid eyes on a porcupine before.

"We see them rarely enough down south that we can tell there aren't any breeding populations here. They're not unheard of, but definitely more common in the north."

"What information do you have about them?" Guy pressed. "Are they an unusual species in any way?"

"Doesn't look like it," Sonny said.

"Yeah," Awsk confirmed. "Their cheat seems to be regeneration, since multiple units have seen them get back up from fatal injuries looking fresh."

Guy's brow furrowed as Awsk showed them more photos and videos of the porcupines in action. They were just as aggressive as every hostile Wellspring creature Guy had seen, and they all looked bigger and meaner than Bea. One particularly graphic video showed one batting a rider off their dragon and then stomping them to death.

"This isn't what she's like at all," Guy said. "I mean, it's definitely the same species, but ... "

"Just seems like your run-of-the-mill stupid, violent monster," Sonny said. "Don't see any reason why it would be special."

"She *is*, though," Guy insisted. "I can't emphasize this enough, she kept me alive even though there was no real reason to do so, as far as I could tell. She brought me food. She can understand spoken words to an extent like the dragons can."

General Hobby was thinking very hard.

"Well, what should we do about it?" Sonny said.

"We should leave soon," General Hobby said slowly, "if we want to go meet her before it gets too dark."

***

Patches was the oldest dragon at Wasp Nest and therefore the largest, having cleared out the space of several honeycombs and destroyed the barriers between them, so he had enough room to curl up. Lucifer, the second-in-command's dragon, often spent his nights curled up and nuzzled into Patches's side. They both dwarfed Bonnie, and he really hoped their overwhelming size didn't make Bea too nervous. Bonnie could probably fit on one of Patches's outstretched wings.

"Up and at 'em, old boy," General Hobby said.

Patches cracked an eye open and glared at him.

"Sorry, I know it's bedtime, but there's something important we have to do. It won't take long, promise."

Patches whined and moaned, dramatically stretching. Lucifer raised his head with bleary eyes, disgruntled at having his drowsing disturbed.

"Saddle on."

Patches continued to grumble, but he crawled over to the area where General Hobby had the stepladder he used to saddle him. The general tightened the straps and then hauled himself up. "Is your saddle too damaged to fly?"

"No, me and Bonnie are okay on that front. My mic is kaput, though, so you'll have to shout loud."

General Hobby lowered his visor. "Got it."

All the dragons began chirping and barking as Patches scaled the wall, too big to even spread his wings to take off inside. He came out on the lip of the roost, spreading his massive wingspan and lifting off, buffeting the topmost dragons quite rudely. Bonnie flitted up behind him, drafting on his tailwind.

Guy really, really hoped that Patches didn't scare Bea. General Hobby was generally pretty easy to talk to, and Guy knew he would be interested in Bea, but his attitude might be different if he couldn't be convinced Bea was safe to be around.

Bonnie led the way to the rocky alcove where Bea had hidden. She touched down amidst Patches's shadow, the huge wyvern coming down after her and leaning over to examine the ground where Bonnie was scuttling around.

"Bea!" Guy called. "It's me! I promise it's safe! We won't hurt you! This is my – my friend! I know he's really big, but –   but he's nice like Bonnie is! Promise!"

Bea's face appeared amidst the sandstone, looking at Patches warily. Patches, unlike Bonnie, was large enough that Bea barely registered as a threat. He merely thrashed his tail and grunted in her direction.

"I see her, boy," General Hobby said. He patted the dragon's flank and pulled the reins back slightly, indicating *stand down*. "It's all right. No need to get agitated. Don't attack."

Patches seemed happy to not have to do something, so he laid down with his belly flat against the ground.

Bonnie trotted over and raised the feathers on her head, trilling at Bea. Bea slowly crept out, not taking her eyes off Patches.

"This is General Hobby and Patches. They're in charge of keeping everyone safe here. They want to meet you."

Bea kept low to the ground and slunk to Bonnie's side. Guy dismounted, coming over and putting a hand on Bea's snout. "See? No fighting. Nothing to worry about."

Bea's eyes flickered around Patches.

"Fascinating," General Hobby said. He slid out of his saddle and down to the ground, approaching slowly. "My name is Jairus," he announced cautiously. "Lieutenant Reed told me you saved his life."

Bea snorted and nervously flicked her head.

"I owe you for bringing him back. He's a fine rider. It would have been a shame to lose him."

Bea crept closer, out from Bonnie.

"General, can she stay here at the station? I don't want anything to happen to her. We usually have leftover food, anyway."

It couldn't be that easy, could it? Just walking up and asking?

But apparently it was. "Yes. I think the folks at Paramount will be interested in her, so we should make sure she's around."

***

Bea herself took some convincing once they got close enough to the station.

She seemed to accept Patches same as she'd accepted Bonnie, and she walked under their wings as they flew without issue.

When all the other humans came into view, along with the errant dragon circling, she started to get more nervous.

As they approached the stables, Bea started to fidget and low at the dragons gathered feeding on the corpses outside the ground floor. The dragons, in turn, raised their heads and barked with interest, nervously jostling and posturing, showing their teeth.

"All right, all right," Guy said. "Come on, now. We're all friends."

The other dragons didn't seem convinced. Bea didn't either, not moving any closer.

Patches, by contrast, spontaneously decided that he was very annoyed with everyone else and moved towards the kill pile, grunting and lashing his tail. The smaller dragons hissed at him, but backed up as he approached. Patches unfurled a wing and decked the boldest member of the group, scattering them amongst outraged honks.

Patches lay down and nibbled at the kill pile, getting a mouthful of meat and swallowing it down. Bonnie trilled and followed him, staying low to the ground as a sign of submission and tiptoeing forwards to also take a few bites. Patches allowed her.

"Are you hungry, Bea?" Guy said. "Go ahead if you want."

Still keeping a nervous eye on Patches, Bea slunk over, keeping her spikes oriented between her and Patches. She stretched her neck out to take the foot of one of the dead creatures, sliding it further away from Patches and towards herself. Patches ignored her, completely disinterested.

"Can we move her into the stables?" Guy asked.

"Yes," the general said. "That's probably the best place for her. If Patches is calm, the rest of the flock should accept her."

Bea ate considerably more than either of the dragons, more even than her bulky frame would suggest. Maybe she was nervous about the next time she would be able to eat, or maybe she was more underfed than he'd guessed.

"There you go, girl," Guy said, patting Bea on the flank. "You took care of me, so I'm gonna take care of you."

When all three beasts had eaten their fill, General Hobby led Patches into the stables. Guy encouraged Bonnie to follow, then kept his hand on Bea's snout. "Do you wanna go inside?"

Bea kept her head low and let out a moo.

"Stay close to Bonnie if you get nervous."

Guy kept his hand on her as he walked inside the shelter. In the dim light of the sunset shining in from the top, the rest of the dragons could be seen peering out from their nests. A few of them growled at her. Bea hunkered down under their glares.

"Go stand by Patches," Guy said. "So everyone sees you're with us."

Bea crept forwards and crouched in Patches's shadow. Patches snorted and sniffed her, then sat down, tucking his limbs under his chest. Bonnie came up on his other side and started to groom his feathery head crest, which he allowed her to do with eyes sliding shut.

"Everyone, this creature is Bea," General Hobby shouted up. "She will be staying here for a little while. Let's keep everything nonviolent."

The rest of the dragons slowly went back to snoozing.

"Bonnie, I'll bring the vet out to check you over tomorrow morning, all right?" Guy was really looking forwards to getting his own medical care, a real shower, and a rest in a real bed.

Bonnie leaned down and licked him.

"Bea, I'll be back out in the morning, okay?"

She grunted.

Guy turned and walked towards the exit. He heard the sound of a heavy creature moving behind him, and felt something gently pulling him backwards.

Bea had very gingerly taken the back of his shirt in her teeth. When he gave her a questioning look, she dropped it and looked at the ground.

Guy smiled and turned back to her, scratching behind her jaw. "You okay?"

She let out an anxious whine.

He patted her snout. "Okay. How about I come back in and sleep in the stables with you and BonBon tonight?"

She pressed her forehead into him.

7

— • —

She'd started to think of herself as Bea, just because Guy called her that.

She'd had a name, she thought. She already had a name, from before. She couldn't remember what it was. She couldn't remember a lot of things from before.

She liked the name, though. Bea. It was small and nice and pretty, everything she wasn't anymore.

Guy wanted her to stay in this weird building full of dragons, and she didn't like that idea at all. She wouldn't be able to fight them off if they got mad at her. When aerial predators attacked, all she could ever do was hunker down with her spikes out to keep them from hitting her. That didn't work for ones who could do things like breathe fire, though.

Bonnie could protect Guy better than she could. Bea secretly hated Bonnie, but it was only because of jealousy. Bonnie had been able to save Guy from falling to his death, and Bea couldn't do anything against aerial predators except save herself.

At first she thought he'd lied about coming back out with how long he was gone. Bea waited by the door, hating the fact that she was too big to fit through and go after him. Who knew what was going on beyond that door? Were the others mistreating him while he was helpless, without even Bonnie to protect him? Were they killing him to eat?

But no. He came back eventually. His hurt foot was in a brand-new boot, and he was walking more easily. He also smelled a lot cleaner, and she could smell he'd eaten – good food, not the raw, inedible meat she'd so stupidly tried to give him.

It was a miracle he even wanted her around anymore. She was stupid and ugly and dangerous and unlike Bonnie, she couldn't even fly. He didn't need her anymore.

Despite that, he came over and patted her snout. "Miss me?"

Yes.

Bonnie's head snaked around and nudged him from the other side. She nearly pushed him over with her nudging, and he laughed and pushed her back.

Bea wanted to hold Guy so badly, but her claws were too big. Every way she had to pick him up would hurt him. She flexed her claws, imagining for a moment that she could use them to cradle him without tearing his skin.

"You good, Bee?"

She grunted.

"The vet's going to come out, okay? He's the one who takes care of our dragons, so he's going to take care of you   too."

She sat down with her limbs tucked under herself. Her defensive position. She was nervous. What if the vet didn't like what it saw? What if it saw that Bea was weird and dangerous, and it told Guy to send her away or kill her?

What *was* a vet, anyway? She couldn't remember what the word meant. Guy was talking about it like it was a doctor, though.

If the vet was a threat, she could probably kill it, unless it was bigger than the dragons.

It turned out to be a second man. She didn't like this one as much. It was uglier. It was bald, instead of having a nice strip of hair she could think about tugging on like Guy. Nevertheless, its words were kind as it directed Bea to stand up, move her limbs, open her mouth. The vet seemed pleased and surprised by her cooperation and told Guy that Bea seemed perfectly healthy and didn't need any medical care.

Maybe that could be her advantage over Bonnie. She didn't need medical care, but Bonnie obviously did if they needed a whole vet to take care of the dragons. Bea couldn't remember any time when she'd needed medical care.

"How ya feeling, girl? All good?"

Bea grunted and leaned into Guy's proffered hand.

"Good. We're gonna just hang out here for a little while then, okay?"

Bea sat as close to Bonnie as she could without hurting any-one with her spikes.

***

Guy slept nestled in Bonnie's wing, and Bea watched them both with burning jealousy.

The next morning was easy and slow and calm. Guy lavished attention on Bonnie. He took her down to the base of the nesting structure and sprayed Bonnie with a hose. Bonnie tried to bite the spray of water, and after they were done, she sat preening her wet feathers.

"Do you want to be hosed off too, Bea?"

Bea grunted and shuffled forwards. She couldn't really keep herself clean, and things accumulated between her spikes. The only time she'd ever get clean was going to the river like she'd done with Guy, but it was too far out of the way to travel there just for that. Just so she could feel clean.

She felt clean now, though, as Guy power washed all the accumulated dirt and muck and grime off her back, her thick skin keeping her from even feeling the pressure very much. Guy had her lift up her paws and washed her claws too, which felt like a nice massage.

"There we go. You smell a lot better now."

Had she smelled bad? Had she been disgusting? Was that something she should worry about, smelling bad?

Guy didn't seem overly worried about it. "We have some time to kill while Jairus talks to the commander general. Do you want to walk around outside?"

She shuffled excitedly. Being out from under all these dragons would be a relief. She hadn't slept well with their eyes on her.

She followed as he walked outside the building. The landscape was rocky, barren, and open – perfectly defensible for aerial predators. Perfect for the dragons. Very bad for her. Guy didn't seem worried about that either.

He walked around the outside of the nest, pointed out things to her, telling anecdotes. "Bonnie smacked into that tree when she was younger. Got a bit too excited and overshot her landing. That was our first major crash. Luckily I was okay, and well, she was okay, of course. Sometimes when it rains, that basin over there accumulates a small lake and everyone is down there all day like it's a beach party. We get flash floods sometimes, but we're up on the hill so usually it doesn't cause too many problems. This spot is a great place to sit to watch the dragons eating. They have the cattiest drama sometimes. It's hilarious. Bonnie is too shy for that, though, she always gives up right away when anyone is mean to her. Some of the meaner dragons have a soft spot for her because of how sweet she is, though, so she doesn't get bullied or anything. I'd show you the inside of the base if I could."

The man Guy had been treating as very important came and found him outside. "Lieutenant, the commander general is on his way down. He wants to talk with you this afternoon."

"What?" Guy suddenly seemed very nervous. Did he need Bea to take him away from here? Would she have to fight the commander general if it tried to eat him? "He's coming down here to talk to *me*?"

"Yeah, he wants to see Bea for himself."

Guy shifted from foot to foot. Bea bumped him with her nose, and he smiled at her and rubbed her head. "Okay, thanks, General."

Guy walked away, very deep in thought. Bea followed, giving a concerned rumble.

"The commander general," Guy said to her. "He's a living legend. He's the leader of the whole guild. He's the one who figured out how to tame dragons. He's – he's – he's coming here to talk to *me*?" He tugged on his collar.

Bea eased forwards and nudged her head under Guy's arm. His nervous expression broke into a smile, and he patted her head. "Thanks, Bee. I know you and Bonnie are gonna be there to support me."

She would. She'd wanted nothing more than to take care of him ever since she'd seen him lying broken and endangered on the pavement. It stirred something in her, something she hadn't felt in a long, long time.

8

— · —

Guy was sitting in a honeycomb brushing Bonnie when the commander general showed up.

There was a huge *boom* as something heavy landed on the outside of the stables, and some of the more skittish dragons started calling and took to the skies, funneling out with a flurry of wings.

A very, very large head with cobalt blue feathers peered down into the stables, neck snaking through.

God, Yough was *huge.* Commander General Eckron's dragon was the oldest dragon in existence, the first one hatched during the Tribulation, and dragons never stopped growing for as long as they lived. Guy had seen the enormous beast occasionally during his training at Paramount, mostly in the form of his colossal shadow falling over them as he passed overhead.

Yough's enormous black eyes looked directly at Guy as he turned his head, peering down. God, one of his eyes was probably as big as Guy's entire head.

"Commander, Commander General," Guy squeaked, then realized he hadn't talked loudly enough to be heard over the din of the stables. "Commander General!"

Commander General Eckron's voice boomed out with mechanical amplification. "Lieutenant. Come meet me outside, why don't you?"

Okay, thank God. Guy wasn't sure Yough would even fit in the stables. "Yes, sir!"

Guy scrambled to put down the brush he'd been using on Bonnie, patting his pockets, trying to think if he needed anything. He picked the brush back up and put it in his pocket, then put it back down again. "Bonnie, can we go down there?"

He didn't stop to put her saddle and bridle on, just jumping on and directing Bonnie down to Bea. "Bee, we're gonna go outside, okay?"

Bea was bristling in the corner, spikes turned outwards, clearly on edge by Yough's recent appearance.

"The commander general wants to meet you. We're just gonna talk, okay? His dragon is really, really big, but he's not gonna hurt you. He's friendly." He didn't know that for sure. Yough's eyes looked mean.

Bea crept forward.

"There you go. Come on."

Bea followed obediently as Bonnie took Guy outside. Yough was roosted on the ground outside, and Eckron was casually leaning against his flank.

"Commander General!" Guy said. He pulled up and slid off Bonnie's back. God, Bonnie was like a kitten next to Yough. The smaller dragon crouched fearfully, not moving any closer.

Eckron flipped his visor up, revealing his salt-and-pepper bearded face. "Riding bareback, are we?"

"Yes, sir! Sorry, sir! I won't do it again, sir!"

Eckron smirked. "Relax. I just think it takes a lot of skill to direct a dragon in flight without a bridle. You have quite a bond."

Stupid, stupid, Guy was being stupid. Stupid, dumb, idiot. "Thank you, sir!"

"Not to mention it means you have no fear of falling off."

"Thank you, sir!"

"It's handling skills like that that make me – "

"Thank you, sir! Oh, sorry, sir! Please, go on, sir!"

"That's quite all right. Just relax now. I was saying you seem trustworthy."

"I'm a trustworthy guy, sir!" Oh no, had he really just made one of his stupid jokes to *the commander general?*

Luckily Eckron seemed to find it funny. "Yes, I suppose you are. That's why I trust you know what you're talking about when you say you found an unusual Wellspring creature."

Guy swallowed nervously. "Yes, sir. We've been calling her Bea."

"Jairus told me she saved your life and brought you and Bonnie back when you were left for dead out by the ruins of Memphis."

"Yes, sir."

Eckron looked past him to Bea, who was hunkered down behind Guy. "It's a pleasure to meet you."

Bea shuffled her feet nervously.

"She certainly does behave more like the dragons than like the other Wellspring creatures."

"She really does. Nobody has any idea why."

"Right ... It's certainly unusual." Eckron stroked his beard. "She responds to verbal commands and gestures the way the dragons do?"

"Mostly, yeah." Guy stepped to the side and gently coaxed Bea forward. "Come on, it's all right."

Bea nervously stepped forward, tail flicking.

"She's nervous around all the dragons, I think."

"Logical. They're quite scary." Eckron held his hand out. "Friendly, are you?"

Bea crept up to his hand at an agonizing pace, sniffing it suspiciously, tail lashing.

Eckron put his hand on her nose. She snorted and bobbed her head, but didn't pull away.

"Interesting. Very interesting." Eckron withdrew his hand. "This is certainly an anomaly worth attention. It could lead to some ... interesting discoveries. Dr. Zhao has been bugging me about some theories she wants to test – she's been pleading with me to let her take a Wellspring creature to the hawk wyvern Wellspring. Bea could help with that. Lieutenant Reed, I'd like for you and Bonnie to help me escort this creature up to Paramount."

"Yes, sir!" Guy choked out. "Yes, absolutely! Sir!"

Eckron waved a hand, clearly starting to get a little annoyed. "All right, at ease, soldier. I'll talk to Jairus about making the preparations and we can set off first thing tomorrow morning."

***

Eckron decided that Major Sinervo would escort them back to Paramount.

That was ... something. Major Sinervo was ... something.

As the only major at Wasp Nest, he was theoretically in charge just behind General Hobby and Colonel Quinn, but usually the more junior riders around him took on the role of babysitters more than subordinates. No one had ever gotten killed following his orders, but missions inevitably took a lot longer when Sinervo was there.

It was an unspoken consensus that Sinervo had only been promoted up as far as he had because of his dragon, Raki. Raki was a freakish anomaly among dragons, huge as a general's dragon without being nearly as old, albino with white feathers and pale red eyes, and wicked smart. Probably smarter than the man strapped to his back. Raki could do most of Sinervo's missions by himself; Sinervo could be swapped out for a training dummy and it probably wouldn't affect their performance at all. It was remarkable Raki managed to get as far as he did with such an idiot pinned to him.

Eckron and Guy waited on the runway, Yough and Bonnie saddled up and ready to go. Bea waited down below, peering up at them and waiting for her cue to follow.

"You're sure he knows he's coming?" Guy said.

"Yes," Eckron said, exasperated.

Guy had asked Sonny to fix the comm in his helmet, so thankfully he was now able to take action to ask about what was going on. He sighed and touched the mic in his helmet. "Hey, Sonny?"

"Tech support?" said Sonny's voice.

"Do you know where Major Sinervo is?"

"Uh ... he's scheduled to be on the runway with you and the commander general five minutes ago."

" ... Right. Thanks."

Raki slithered up out of the stables, grunting and chuffing. He wasn't even wearing his saddle yet.

"Good morning, Raki," Guy said.

Raki growled and tapped his claws on the stone of the runway.

Bonnie trilled and raised her head crest at him.

Raki threw back his head, opened his mouth to show his rows of icicle-like teeth, and let out a bone-jarring roar.

A few seconds later, the door to the castle flew open and Major Sinervo came out, dragging a saddle behind him. "Sorry, sorry, here I am."

He threw the saddle onto Raki, whose tail was swishing irritably, and started doing up the straps. "Well, then, I'm here now, so we can be off on our special mission! Let's get going!"

The second Sinervo's feet touched the stirrups, Raki stood and bounded away, seemingly without consideration for his rider's readiness or lack thereof. Sinervo was still trying to do up the leg straps as Raki tossed himself off the cliff and into the open air.

Bonnie followed, swooping down low enough that Guy could signal to Bea to follow. Bea gave a moo and broke into a gallop.

"We'll probably want to roost for a short rest after about an hour," Guy said into his comm. "Bea can't run for much longer than that without needing to stop, as far as I can tell."

"I don't suppose we can just pick her up?" Sinervo said. "Ol' Raki is certainly big enough to carry her."

Guy looked down at Bea, a hunk of spikes kicking up a dust cloud to follow. " ... I don't think she'd like that very much."

"Aw, come on, Lieutenant, you never know until you try!"

" ... I think I know on this one, Major. Respectfully."

Storm clouds were gathering on the horizon, but Guy wasn't worried. With someone as experienced as Commander General Eckron, he had no doubt whatsoever they would make it to Paramount safely. Raki being here was nice extra insurance in case they ran into any Wellspring creatures.

"What's the agenda when we get to Paramount?" Sinervo said.

"We'll have Dr. Zhao examine Bea and give us her assessment. Since Bea is so unusual, we'll want to catalog her as a case report in the archives. After that, we'll take her to the Wellspring by Paramount."

"What for, Commander General?" Sinervo broke in.

There was silence for a moment, Yough's wings flapping. Guy could feel disapproval radiating from Eckron. "Major Sinervo. Wellsprings are the source of magic that Wellspring creatures draw from, so an unusual creature like Bea might have a reaction to a Wellspring."

"Uh-huh," said Sinervo.

Tense silence filled the communications line. Guy wanted to pipe up and ask if everything was okay, but he was too scared. He'd never seen anyone interact with Eckron this way before.

The conversation was light after that, and eventually Guy noticed Bea starting to lag behind and called for them to take a break. The dragons found an open space to land on, and Bea followed, panting.

"You're doing great," he told her, patting her side.

Bea's tongue was lolling out of her mouth when she reached them, and Guy held his hand on her nose. "Can we find some water nearby?" Despite the clouds, sweat rolled down his back. He could only imagine Bea and the dragons would appreciate some water.

"I'll go scout for some," Sinervo said.

"Be careful," Eckron told him. "We've had recent reports of poxies in the area."

Raki took off.

"How ya holding up, girl?" Guy said, rubbing Bea's head.

Bea gave a nervous moan and shuffled closer to him.

"You're doing great. We're going to a bigger station, and there will be more food and more people to meet there."

She shifted from foot to foot, jittery.

"Me and Bonnie will be with you. Nothing bad is gonna happen to you there."

She crouched down on the ground, flicking her ears and bobbing her head.

Sinervo came back and reported a shallow watering hole nearby, so they moved over there. Bonnie lay down and stuck her snout into the water.

"We should be safe enough from poxies," Guy offered. "They usually need more shadow than this to manifest in any decent numbers." The overcast sky meant shadows were ill-defined and weak.

Eckron scanned the horizon. "Safe enough."

Raki had been circling in the air but now came back at top speed, touching down and sliding to a stop and kicking up a huge cloud of dirt, panting. "Commander, there's something over there! Under the storm clouds."

Guy looked in the indicated direction, squinting. "Awsk?"

"Let me get a closer look at it." Awsk took control of the zoom function on Guy's visor and focused on the area beneath the roiling clouds. A huge creature jumped into focus, one with long, knobby limbs and an impressive set of antlers. The entire creature glowed soft blue, and sparks danced around its antlers, the occasional jolt of electricity arcing between the points. Despite its resemblance to a very large, twisted deer, its mouth hung open in a predatory snarl.

"Lightning elk," Awsk said.

"Shit." Guy swung back into Bonnie's saddle. "That could be a problem." This was one of the strictly terrestrial Wellspring creatures that it was nevertheless not safe to fight from the air. Being closer to the sky put you in better range of its primary weapon.

Unlike natural lightning, the elk's lightning would go wherever the creature directed it rather than anything to do with heights or magnetism, so they couldn't even try to make a lightning rod to keep themselves safe. It had to aim, though, so if they kept moving, it would have a harder time hitting them. If they kept low to the ground –

Thunder clapped as a bolt of lightning streaked down and absorbed into the elk's antlers. The flash of bright light threw shadows all around and –

Ah, symbiotic hunters. Smart.

The poxies erupted out of the shadows a moment later, all snarling teeth and claws. Guy unsheathed his knife and stabbed it into the one that had leapt at him, its blood spraying out and adding more red to its already crimson fur coat. "Commander?!"

Yough picked Eckron up and tossed him into the saddle. "Sinervo, go deal with the elk! Guy and I will protect Bea."

"Right!" Sinervo said. "Up, then, Raki, m'boy, into the sky."

Sinervo tugged the reins up to signal gaining altitude, but Raki snaked his head down and raced forward, staying low to the ground.

"That works too, whatever you're feeling, Raki."

Guy watched nervously as Raki ignored more commands from his rider and approached the elk, but Raki's ideas seemed to be safer than Sinervo's, so maybe that was for the best. He was sure anyone else displaying this level of incompetence in front of Eckron would have been dismissed instantly, but Raki was bonded to Sinervo and likely couldn't be ridden by anyone else, and that dragon was way too valuable to lose. He demonstrated why as he expertly dodged multiple lightning strikes, weaving deftly to attack his prey.

Meanwhile, Bea didn't seem to need much defending; the poxies attacking her couldn't figure out a way past her spikes, and she took them out easily with broad sweeps of her tail. They were small enough to die underfoot.

They were more of a threat to Guy. He kept stabbing until he could get up onto Bonnie's back. Bonnie instinctively lifted off to get them out of danger.

A lightning bolt cracked down a few feet from her, sending her flapping backwards with a startled roar. More poxies appeared in the fresh shadows, and a few of them hopped up onto Bonnie's back and latched onto Guy.

Bonnie swiveled her sinuous neck to try and bite the ones off Guy, but that exposed her neck to the ones in front of her. She roared and reared back as their teeth sunk in.

"Steady, Bon!" Guy shouted. He was having flashbacks to the raptors as the teeth and claws worked at his armor, trying to find his weak spots.

Bea's hulking figure cast a shadow over Guy, and her huge claws swiped at the ones attacking him. She overshot and her swing hit Guy straight in the stomach – it was the flat of her claws and not the point, thank God, or he would have been toast. It knocked the wind out of him and sent him spinning, the saddle sliding slightly as the restraints tried to find a middle ground between keeping him in the saddle and keeping the saddle on Bonnie's back.

"Bee," he gasped, unable to say much more.

Bea let out a worried moan, hugging close to him with her spikes facing the poxies.

Bonnie tried to pull away, clawing at the poxies with her back feet

"Bee, let Bonnie – "

Bea panicked as Bonnie left her and took Guy. She spun around stomping on the poxies and knocking them back, roaring, and then turned tail and ran.

Another bolt of lightning aimed at Eckron thankfully missed, but it did summon even more teeth and claws from the shadows.

"Major!" Eckron yelled into the comms as Yough knocked back his assailants.

"On it! Sorry!"

"Awsk," Guy said, pulling Bonnie's reins to go after Bea. "Any useful info on lightning elk?"

"Hmmm," Awsk said. "So, its antlers are immune to electricity, but the rest of its body isn't. But it knows not to strike itself with lightning anywhere else."

"Major, kite the elk over to the lake," Guy called, keenly aware of how inappropriate it was for him to be giving orders to the major ... but Sinervo didn't seem to have his own plan.

Raki swooped down and dive-bombed the elk, prompting a rapid series of lightning strikes that the dragon expertly dodged.

"Lieutenant, you and I move over the lake," Eckron added.

"Yes," Guy said.

He pulled Bonnie away from where Bea had disappeared to fly low over the water. The poxies followed, splashing in the shallows.

Raki swooped over the elk again, and this time it gave chase. Raki expertly weaved to dodge its bolts, then flew over the water.

The elk's hooves splashed through the shallows around its poxy allies, braying angrily. Guy pulled up further away from the water as a final lightning strike came down and touched the water.

With a crackling sound, all the poxies and the elk convulsed with electricity, then fell dead with the smell of smoking meat.

" ... Whew," Sinervo said.

Yough splashed back down into the shallows, sniffing at the electrified corpses. "Good work, Lieutenant Reed," Eckron said, pointedly not saying anything to Sinervo.

"Good job, Raki," Sinervo said, patting the dragon's side. Raki moaned and rolled his eyes, coming over to join Yough and mouth at the corpses.

"Well, at least that's the dragon's feed for the day sorted out!" Guy said, trying desperately to handle the strange tension building between Eckron and Sinervo. It was way above his rank.

9

— . —

Guy managed to find Bea cowering behind a rock nearby. Her snout had some shallow scratches where apparently the poxies had managed to get past her spikes. She seemed embarrassed, ashamed to come out.

"Oh, sh, sh, it's okay," Guy soothed. He took out a cloth and wiped the blood off her snout. "It's all right. You're okay."

She rumbled and stuck her nose to his chest, quivering.

"I'm okay too. We're all okay. Come get something to eat. There's plenty of bodies around."

Fortunately, their meal and the subsequent rest of the trip to Paramount went without issue. The looming stone castle came into view over the horizon.

"It's been a while for you, hasn't it, Lieutenant?" Eckron said.

"Yes, sir." He hadn't been to the guild headquarters since training.

"Feel free to reminisce. Dr. Zhao isn't going to be available until later today, so we have some time to kill until then."

They touched down on the runway. Guy had Bonnie swoop down to where Bea was still laboriously climbing up the pathway to the summit.

"You good?"

She grunted, seemingly embarrassed that she couldn't fly.

Bonnie landed and folded her wings in. "We'll go together, how about that?"

Bea perked up a little bit, stepping with renewed vigor.

When Bonnie slithered up onto the runway, a chorus of voices greeted him, riders he'd been beside in training that had stayed at Paramount instead of being shipped off to a point station.

"Guy! Hey, it's Guy!"

"That's *Lieutenant Guy* to you! I'm an important guy, you know!"

"Haven't changed a bit, I see."

I really have, and not for the better.

"Word on the street is you have a new pet monster."

"It's true, so you better be nice to me before I sic her on you."

"Ooooh, *her*, is it? You finally lucky in love?"

"Come on, I already made tender love to your mother and we all know she has the face of a monster."

This prompted a smattering of laughter. Guy secretly thought these people were extremely stupid, but the only way to get them to leave you alone was to play along, make them laugh, and then disappear as fast as possible. A joke about one's mother was just enough to get the job done, and he was able to get them to leave him alone long enough to make sure Bea was settled in and not too scared of the dragons in the stables.

The Paramount stables were much nicer, big enough for the oldest dragons to nest in. He found Bea a nice cavern tucked into the wall down on the ground. Bea seemed most comfortable when she could hunker down out of sight.

"This okay for now?"

Bea bobbed her head and flicked her ears.

"Bonnie will stay here with you. I'm going to go get some lunch, okay?"

She grunted. Bonnie came over and started licking her head, which seemed to annoy her.

"Lieutenant Reed!" someone shouted above him from dragonback. "Rainer heard you were going to be at Paramount today and begged me to get you to come help him train the new recruits!"

Guy sighed and tried to hide his expression, fixing his face into an enthusiastic grin before turning back. "Oh, that sounds great! Sure, when?"

"Today's hatching and matching for the new squads, so whenever you can get to the stables!"

***

He had fond memories of Rainer and the people who'd hatched Bonnie. They were kind, patient, and helpful to a fault. The only thing they cared about was making sure the dragons were taken care of – their babies. Guy hoped that one day he'd be able to do that – not until Bonnie had passed, though. None of the hatchery workers had dragons of their own.

"Trainer Rainer!" Guy shouted with glee, coming into the training center. Rainer was the one who'd given him instructions on how to bond with Bonnie. They barely knew each other, but Rainer was like an old friend to Guy.

"Sorry, who's that?" Rainer said with feigned ignorance. "I don't remember who you are. You look like just some guy!"

The students all groaned as Rainer and Guy clasped hands, grinning.

"So, Rainer, I've been told these new recruits are meeting their dragons today?" Guy started.

"You bet! I was hoping you'd have some words for them."

Guy suddenly felt very serious, his stomach dropping. *Did* he have words for them?

What would *he* say?

To a bunch of *kids*?

He looked out over their eager faces. They looked the same as the ones that'd been crushed under that building that nearly took him out. Identical. Even though he couldn't remember the faces of the ones that had died.

He hadn't gotten attached, not at all –

The kids never last –

"Don't die," he said, and was horrified to find his voice thick with emotion. He cleared his throat and swallowed the tears. "Don't die," he said again, voice steadier. "It's tempting to get caught up in all the glory and excitement, but I promise you it's more impressive to survive than it is to die in a blaze of glory. Your dragon is going to be your best friend, and they're depending on you to survive."

"Well put," Rainer said. "Now, Lieutenant Reed is going to join us in the hatchery. It's always a reason for celebration when we have a successful clutch of newborns."

The hatchery was deep in the protected belly of Paramount, well away from the stables, since they couldn't risk the adults attacking the newborns. It was a dungeon-like room with stone walls, shrouded in quiet darkness, and everyone whispered as though in the presence of something holy.

He wished Bonnie were here.

The air lit up with the cheeping of dragon chicks. The newborns were fresh and wet, gangly creatures with limp feathers sitting among their eggshells looking confused. They looked oddly humanoid here, this small and this undeveloped. A barely bipedal creature with wings like arms sprouting feathers, an animalistic snout in place of a face, a tail to balance out the heavy back legs, balancing on feet sprouting claws they did not know how to use. A few of them were screaming at the horror of being brought to life.

Relatable.

***

Dr. Zhao was finally available. She was one of the few people at Paramount Guy had never met. She was important, gravely so, since she was the foremost expert on Wellspring science. She'd been the one to identify the mechanism of Wellspring creatures' near-immortality. She'd been there to help Eckron raise the first brood of dragons.

She rarely appeared in public. She would only show up when Eckron asked her to, and sometimes not even then.

There was no mistaking her, though. A petite, graying woman moving far faster than would be expected of someone her age. Her leg bounced as she stood in place. "Where is the creature, then?"

"Down here," Guy said. He leaned over the ledge and beckoned Bea up. "Come on. Want to meet the nice doctor?"

Bea shyly crawled up, staying low to the ground.

"Ah," Zhao said. She took a screen out of her pocket and pulled it open, the glassy surface flashing with images as she used her thumbs to navigate it. "A porcupine, certainly. Underdeveloped."

"She's smart, though," Guy said. "Smarter than even – " He stopped as he realized Zhao wasn't even listening to him.

She'd pulled up an entry about porcupines and projected a holographic image of their typical appearance, comparing them with her eyes bouncing back and forth. Just as Guy had seen before, the image was bigger, meaner, more savage, more spikes.

"Ah," Zhao said. "This is a first-generation. That explains it."

"First-generation … ?" Guy said.

Zhao manipulated the images floating above her screen with a series of rapid-fire finger movements, leg still bouncing. "Creatures born directly from Wellsprings are smaller and more docile. Once they establish breeding populations, their phenotype changes. It's a phenomenon called form progression."

"Form progression … " Guy echoed. "Um, okay."

Zhao didn't elaborate, rapidly typing on her electronic device.

"You've faced feral hawk wyverns before, right?" Eckron offered. "They looked different from our domestic ones, didn't they?"

"Oh, yeah," Guy said, realization dawning. They'd been bigger, faster, and far more aggressive. "I'd wondered why they were like that, but everyone told me that's just what feral wyverns were like."

"Our dragons are all first generation. Their eggs are pulled directly out of the Wellspring. Second generation wyverns are too temperamental to train for riding."

"We've tried," Zhao cut in.

Guy had never seen eggs come from Wellsprings before. He knew theoretically that was where Wellspring creatures came from, but he'd only heard about it from the riders who came back laden with new eggs for the hatchery. "Okay," Guy said. "So Bea is rare because she came directly out of a Wellspring, then?"

Bea pressed her forehead into Guy, and he put his hand on her ear and rubbed. "What does that mean, then?"

Zhao snapped her screen shut and put it in her pocket. "Dunno. I'll meet you at the Wellspring tomorrow morning, though. Bye."

She walked out.

"Um," Guy said. "Okay. Thanks."

***

When Guy didn't know something, he went to the library. And there was a lot he didn't know.

He checked out one of the screens, going to one of the docks and contemplatively browsing the archives. Hand on chin and deep in thought, he flipped through pages about Wellsprings. Wellspring creatures, Wellspring phenomena. The eggs that came out of Wellsprings, and hatched into monsters that bore children that became even more monstrous.

What was the difference between a creature from a Wellspring and one born to Wellspring creatures?

He couldn't find an answer. If anyone would know, it would be Zhao, right? She hadn't seemed at all interested in it, though.

He looked up Zhao's biography. She had studied molecular genetics before the Tribulation, apparently. Her name was on dozens of academic papers about cytokines and aquaporins and interleukins. Guy lost interest before he could fall too far down that rabbit hole. It was way too complicated to understand.

Her biography said how she'd met Eckron. She'd heard of his project to try and tame Wellspring creatures and joined up with his group to establish what eventually became the guild.

There was a picture, from the early days of the Tribulation. Eckron, looking much younger and with more hair, kneeling with General Hobby and General Lively, along with Zhao, also looking much younger. There were three people he didn't recognize. The caption read:

Lawrence Eckron, Jairus Hobby, Amotz Lively, Wei Zhao, Alastair Yough, Raki Kaya, Ansel Müller, 2072.

Yough had been a close associate of Eckron's during the Tribulation; everyone knew about him even though he'd died during the Tribulation because Eckron's dragon was named after him. And Sinervo's dragon was named after Raki, although Guy didn't know anything about him. Ansel Müller was a name he'd never heard before, either human or dragon.

Yough was an imposing man with a very serious face. Ansel was a young woman with long, brown hair. Raki was ... tall. The tallest in the group. And he looked like he had albinism. His eyes were pale pink. Guy stared at him, thinking very hard.

"Lieutenant Reed."

Guy jumped, clutching his chest and looking over at who'd spoken. It was Sinervo. "Hello, Major."

"Doing some reading, are we?"

He put his head in his hand and flipped the screen closed. "Just realizing there's a lot I don't know."

"That's true for all of us. At least you realize it." Sinvero looked around nervously and then leaned in. "You can't go to the Wellspring tomorrow with Eckron."

Guy furrowed his brow. "Why not?"

Sinervo shifted from foot to foot. "If I told you – "

"You'd have to kill me? Come on." Guy plugged the glass tablet back into its socket and started walking.

Sinervo hesitated, then followed and whispered. "Take Bea and leave. Run from the guild. Go south."

"No offense, Major, but I'd listen to the commander general over you."

Guy left Sinervo standing there directionless in the library.

10

—•—

Guy's eyes bounced from Eckron in front of him, mounted on Yough's huge shoulders as they flew, down to Bea running in front of a dust cloud underneath them.

"General?" Guy said hesitantly.

"Yes, Lieutenant?"

"Permission to speak freely?"

"Granted."

"What are we going to the Wellspring for?"

"To meet Zhao for some research."

"But what exactly will we be doing there? It won't hurt Bea, will it?"

Yough's wings flapped. "No," Eckron said slowly. "It won't hurt Bea."

A pit of anxiety formed in Guy's stomach. "How is Zhao getting there? Is she meeting us?"

"She's being escorted by General Lively."

Guy looked back at the sky behind them – empty. No other dragons following. "When?"

"They'll be behind us shortly. No need to worry about the logistics, Lieutenant, I have it all sorted out."

If Guy had been given less time, he wouldn't have paid Major Sinervo's words much mind. But as it stood, with a trip to the Wellspring in silence, Guy had nothing to do but second-guess himself.

It was too late for that, though. If for some reason he'd wanted to take Sinervo's insane advice for no reason at all, peeling off now would raise a lot of questions from Eckron, and he couldn't outrun Yough.

The Wellspring came into view: the guild had built an iron structure around it to keep it safe, since it was critical to the guild's function. It was empty now, though Eckron informed him it was quite lively around egg-production season.

"Roaming Wellspring creatures would have no reason to mess with this Wellspring, as far as we know, but we keep it secured anyway just in case."

"So this is where all the Wellspring creatures came from?"

"Good heavens, no. Each species has their own individual Wellspring. They're scattered across the globe. I'm not surprised you didn't know that, though. It's not common knowledge anymore ... This one is just for the hawk wyverns."

Eckron landed and dismounted, approaching the door. Guy had Bonnie touch down, then turned to watch Bea catch up. Bea was panting when she arrived.

"Good job, girl," Guy told her. "You're doing great."

Bea gave a lopsided smile and rumbled happily, laying flat out on the ground.

"Lieutenant, let's make sure there aren't any eggs inside before we let Bea in. Sometimes the wyverns will smash the eggs or attack juveniles."

Right, wyvern eggs were a precious commodity they couldn't risk. "Okay, sir. I'll wait here with Bea."

"I'll need you to help me carry the egg if there is one inside."

Guy still sat in Bonnie's saddle, glad his visor was hiding his expression. Eckron stood there waiting for him to come over. Guy was doing calculations about whether or not he could take Eckron in a fight, whether or not Bonnie and Bea could take Yough in a fight, and he didn't like the results he kept getting.

"Yes, sir." Guy slowly untethered himself from Bonnie's saddle and slid down. Bonnie, sensing his anxiety, nudged him. "It's all right, girl, just wait here and watch Bea, yeah?"

Bea flicked her ears and bobbed her head.

"Just wait there and watch Bonnie, okay?"

Eckron used his fingerprint to open the lock on the door, and Guy followed him inside.

It was dark inside, with only reinforced glass from the high vaulted ceiling letting in some sunlight. Guy could hear running water, and as his eyes adjusted to the darkness, he saw the Wellspring itself: a pond with a gentle current, a small spring bubbling up from the center. Not what he'd expected. All told, it was pretty underwhelming.

"So this is where all the wyvern eggs come from?" Guy said.

"Yes. Some unknown force we are still researching deep underground is connected to Wellsprings across the planet, fueling the Wellspring creatures through this water."

"Well, there aren't any eggs, so we can have – "

The door shut and locked mechanically. Sweating, Guy walked over and tried his fingerprint to open it. As he'd feared, it didn't work.

"No need to be nervous, Lieutenant," Eckron said, taking his jacket off.

"Why are we really here, Commander?" Guy said. His eyes darted around the room – the only thing he could think of was that Eckron was going to drown him, or bash him over the head with a rock, and neither of those made very much sense.

Bonnie gave a nervous little yowl from outside.

"I'm here to tell you something that very, very few people in the guild know, Lieutenant. There's a reason the wyverns all have to be first-generation."

Don't tell me. Don't tell me, because then you'll have to kill me.

"The Wellsprings produce eggs for us, but to do that the Wellsprings ... have to be fed."

"Commander General, why are you telling me this?"

"Because I want to give you the chance to do this willingly. People that go into this process kicking and screaming make for particularly uncooperative dragons during training."

Guy's fear instantly ratcheted up to maximum, suddenly piecing together a *lot* of pieces he suddenly wished he hadn't seen.

"No," he said. "No, no, it can't be true. You're – you're a *hero*, you tamed the dragons. You haven't been *throwing people into the Wellspring* to do that, have you?"

Eckron held out his hand. "Come on, Lieutenant. The guild would fall apart if everyone knew, so we have to keep it secret. You know too much to continue serving the guild as a rider, but I know you'll make a fine dragon."

"No," Guy said, stumbling backwards, numb. "No, no, no."

"The hard way, then."

"General, wait!" Guy shouted as Eckron seized him. "No, no, wait! Wait! You don't have to do this! Fuck!"

Bonnie and Bea roared from outside, and Yough could be heard stomping around.

Guy unsheathed his knife and tried to stab Eckron, but the blade glanced off the thick armor of the arm dragging him towards the Wellspring.

"I won't tell anyone! I'll be your accomplice!"

"Come on, Lieutenant, don't fight it."

Guy bent over to try and twist out of his grip, and the two men dissolved into wrestling, breathing heavily and cursing at each other.

Bonnie and Yough were clearly getting into it outside, snarling and hissing. Yough suddenly gave a pained sound as though he'd stepped on something sharp, and the wall to Guy's left dented inwards as though hit by a great force.

"Bea!" Guy screamed. "Bea, Bonnie, help!"

The dent came in further under another blow. Bonnie and Yough didn't have the strength to pierce through the metal, but maybe Bea did. She was heavier, spikier, stronger.

A miracle: a third blow split the metal open, and Bea's claw came in, groping blindly. She stuck her face in, but it wasn't wide enough to get into. She disappeared as she backed up for another blow. Bonnie and Yough continued to give outraged howls as they fought each other. Guy prayed for Bea to do this quickly; he knew Bonnie wouldn't last long if that fight kept up.

"Call her off," Eckron demanded, putting Guy in a headlock. "If I die or if word of this gets out, the guild will fall apart and everyone under our protection will die."

"Let go of me! Get off!"

"*Call her off.* You're going to doom humanity a second time."

Metal screeched as the wall split open further as Bea hurled herself at it, and this time it was enough for her to wiggle through, spikes scraping against the metal. She pounced on the two men on the ground, slapping Eckron away and accidentally standing on Guy and knocking the wind out of him.

Bonnie appeared a moment later, also forcing her body through the hole. Yough, far too large to follow, jammed his head in and gave an outraged scream.

"Bee – " Guy wheezed. "Bee, let me up."

Bea removed her crushing foot, and Guy staggered to his feet, leaning on Bea as Bonnie swiftly put herself between him and Eckron.

Guy locked eyes with Eckron. "This whole time," he said, trying not to cry. "You're the one who figured out you had to throw people into a Wellspring to make a dragon you could ride, and you hid that from us."

"I had to!" Eckron said. "Nobody would throw themselves into a Wellspring willingly! If I wanted to harness this to save humanity, it had to stay secret! Even if it meant getting my hands dirty!"

"People would!" Guy argued. "You don't know that! You didn't have to do – *this*!"

Yough's claws scraped against the metal as he tried to peel it back to follow, but he didn't have the same force as Bea.

"It doesn't matter now!" Eckron said. "What's done is done, and we can't have the guild falling apart when we're the only thing standing between us and a second Tribulation!"

"Bea was a person," Guy said, tears now sliding down his cheeks. "And she just got unlucky enough to fall into a Wellspring somewhere out there, didn't she? And she just had to figure out how to deal with that? She just had to figure out how to survive out there among monsters?"

"Lieutenant ... "

"*Bonnie* was a person – a human woman, and you – you did this to her!" Bonnie's head swung around to block him from advancing on Eckron, moaning worriedly. "She was an innocent person and you made her life into a nightmare!"

"A nightmare?" Eckron said. "Come on. She seems happy, don't you think?"

"She doesn't understand what you did to her!" Guy screamed, and now Bea pulled him back, sandwiching him between Bea and Bonnie.

The metal grinded as Yough's claws tore it back a little, then shoved his head in to try and fit again.

"Come on," Eckron said. "It's not too late for you. You can either take this secret to your grave, or you can live on in some way. We'll just say this beast you brought went wild for no reason and had to be put down, and you can still be with Bonnie – closer to her, even. I'll make sure you're assigned together."

"Fuck you!" Guy said. "Fuck you, sir!"

Yough finally managed to get his head in, but when he tried to snap at Bea, he got a faceful of her spikes and pulled back out.

It was then that Bonnie did something that she almost never did: she made an executive decision.

Guy was still a mess, swimming in his revelations and anger at Eckron. Bonnie turned her head sideways, seized him in her jaws, and darted through the opening Yough had just made.

Yough's head snaked around to follow them as Bonnie flitted past, and he spread his wings to take off and give chase. Bea came out next, though, and clamped her jaws around Yough's leg. The wyvern reared back with an outraged bellow.

That was the last Guy saw before they disappeared, swallowed by the rock hurtling past them as Bonnie fled the scene.

***

Guy hadn't been able to stop crying. Bonnie eventually made the effort to find a small stream of water, and she plopped him down into it pointedly with a splash.

"Thank you," he choked out. He turned over and crawled on his hands and knees, splashing his face, still sobbing. The water was cool and clear and felt nice.

He looked up at Bonnie with puffy eyes. She cocked her head, turning one brilliant blue eye towards him.

"This is so messed up," he said. He wobbled to his feet. "Bonnie."

She trilled, raising her head crest.

"I'm sorry, Bonnie. I'm sorry. I didn't know."

Bonnie's eyes followed him as he staggered over and undid her bridle. "I'm sorry," he sobbed. "I'm sorry. I didn't know. I would never have guessed. I'm sorry."

He dropped the bridle into the stream, then undid the saddle, letting it slide off. "You can leave," Guy said. "You didn't choose to be here. You didn't choose to be with me. You didn't choose any of this."

Bonnie trilled in a concerned way and nosed at his hand.

"You don't even understand what's wrong," he wailed. "You can't understand!"

She turned her head sideways, nose in his hand. Her eyes were watery.

Maybe she *did* understand.

"Can you understand what I'm saying right now? Blink twice if you can understand what I'm saying."

She rumbled magnanimously and pulled her head back, nuzzling Guy's shoulders, closing her eyes. She brought her wing around and nestled him in it.

Maybe she didn't. He had no way of knowing.

He did know one thing, though: she had nowhere to go without him. She would be consigned to roaming around the wild like an animal, like Bea had been, if Guy abandoned her. And despite his moral grandstanding, she didn't seem to *want* to leave.

Guy sniffled and took her head in his hands. "If you want to stay, I'm with you for life," he said, voice shaky. "It's you and me, Bonnie. I want it to be your choice, though."

Bonnie leaned down and delicately picked the bridle up with her teeth, setting the dripping implement in Guy's hands.

Guy wiped his face on his arm. "Thank you, Bonnie. Thank you for being here with me. I don't know how to help you understand what's going on, but I'll always take care of you. I'll always do whatever I can to help you."

Bonnie perked up, head turning towards where a heavy thumping sound revealed Bea, claws scraping over the rock to join them in the stream. She was covered in burns and bite marks, blood and embers running down through her spikes.

"Bea," Guy called, rushing over.

She collapsed to the ground, lowing sorrowfully. "Bee," Guy said, cupping her jaws. "Bee, you did so good. Thank you. Thank you for coming to find me."

Her eyes slid closed, and she exhaled slowly.

"Let me help you. I'll get you bandaged up and everything, and – and just like you did for me."

Bonnie came over and covered her with her wings.

Guy put his one hand on her, keeping the other hand on Bea. "We're gonna be okay."

He looked up to the sky, the clouds pink and puffy from the sun. "South, huh?" He never in a million years would have taken Sinervo's advice to flee the guild unless something this drastic had happened to him firsthand.

But now he knew he had no choice. Everyone would believe whatever version of the story Eckron told them, probably that Bea had gone berserk and attacked like he'd said earlier. At best, Guy would have to leave Bea behind for dead and go back to being a rider. With the knowledge of what the dragons really were forever burned in his brain. He could keep killing

Wellspring creatures that had never been human at all, but how could he ever look any dragon in the eye again knowing they'd been drowned, transformed, mindwiped, and made to submit without anyone even knowing what they really were?

How could he possibly just go back to normal after this?

Guy tangled his fingers in the soft feathers of Bonnie's abdomen, using the other hand to reassuringly rub Bea's head. "I'm gonna take care of the two of you. I don't know how, but I'm going to find a way to help you. I promise."

ABOUT THE AUTHOR

Nox is a lover of all creatures and people in sci-fi and fantasy and loves stories about persevering through horrors to come out better on the other side.

— · —

Before You Go

This is the eleventh book in 12 Months of Whump, a series of whumpy novellas published by WPP throughout 2025. Each novella can be read as a standalone.
To stay up to date with the 12 Months of Whump series and other whumperfly-inducing projects, visit us at https://thewhumpyprintingpress.tumblr.com/